THE INNOCENCE GAME

MICHAEL HARVEY

B L O O M S B U R Y

LONDON • NEW DELHI • NEW YORK • SYDNEY

First published in Great Britain 2013

Copyright © 2013 by Michael Harvey

The moral right of the author has been asserted

Bloomsbury Publishing Plc
50 Bedford Square
London
WC1B 3DP

www.bloomsbury.com

Bloomsbury Publishing, London, New Delhi, New York and Sydney

A CIP catalogue record for this book is available from the British Library

ISBN 978 1 4088 3516 6

10 9 8 7 6 5 4 3 2 1

Book design by Michael Collica

Printed and bound in Great Britain by CPI Group (UK) Ltd, Croydon CR0 4YY

THE
INNOCENCE
GAME

Also by Michael Harvey

The Chicago Way
The Fifth Floor
The Third Rail
We All Fall Down

For Mary Frances

THE
INNOCENCE
GAME

PROLOGUE

I sat in the lawyer's office and stared at a row of diplomas on the wall. The writing was impossible to read—a fitting introduction, I figured, to the practice of law. I was about to get up for a closer look at the goods when the man himself came in, small and dark, with soft whispers and greasy handshakes. He sat behind his desk and gestured for me to make myself comfortable. Not likely. He took out a thin blue file, placed it on his desk, and folded his hands over it.

"As you know, Ian, I'm handling your mother's estate."

"I didn't know she had an estate."

"Nearly everyone has an estate, Ian."

"No kidding."

He gave me a nod, like this lesson in and of itself was worth the L ride downtown. "She didn't have a lot, your mother. The house, of course, a little less than five thousand dollars in a savings account, and a small insurance policy to cover her final expenses."

I hadn't thought about final expenses. I was surprised my mom had. As I was about to find out, my mom was full of surprises.

"She left you something else," the lawyer said. "It's the reason I've asked you down here." He took an envelope out of the blue file and turned it over in his hands. "She insisted you read it alone. In this office. Once you've done that, I have an affidavit for you to sign. Then I can release the money."

"Thanks, but you can keep the cash."

The lawyer looked at me like I'd just punched the pope in the stomach. Or some such infallible being. "I can't do that, Ian."

"Have you read it?" I said, nodding at the letter.

"It's sealed. No one's read it but your mom. And now you." He placed the envelope flat on the desk and lifted himself from his chair. "Take your time. When you're done, we'll fill out the paperwork and talk about funeral arrangements."

The lawyer left. I stared at the envelope. I could see my name, hidden in the folds of my mom's cursive, and crumbled a little inside. I pulled the envelope toward me. The paper was thick. Expensive. It felt like a single sheet. Maybe two. I slipped my finger under the edge of the flap and broke the seal. Then I took out the letter and began to read.

I

The seminar met in Fisk Hall, one of the oldest buildings on North-western's campus and the crusted, beating heart of the university's Medill School of Journalism. I took a seat at a table in the back. The pile of red hair at the front shook itself like a dog shaking off the weather. A hand beckoned.

"Won't do, Mr. Joyce."

I sighed, grabbed my backpack, and found a place up front. The pile of hair parted itself, revealing a considerable length of nose and eyes of violent blue.

"My name is Judy Zombrowski. You can call me Z. Do you know Ms. Gold?"

The hand directed my attention to a woman sitting directly to my left. She had a perfectly square chin, high cheekbones, and long, brown hair that turned crimson in the late-afternoon sun. Sarah Gold waved. I felt queasy. Gloriously so.

"We know each other from undergrad," Sarah said, smiling at me as if we'd exchanged more than three words during our four years together.

"Of course you do." Z cast a look toward the back of the room. "We're waiting for one more."

A door banged open.

The third student in the summer graduate seminar was tall and angular. He had thick shoulders and a long jaw covered by a blond scruff of beard. His eyes were shaded and hard to read.

"Jake Havens?" Z's voice rang down the empty aisle and echoed off the walls. Havens took the same seat I'd picked out for myself.

"What is it with you people?" Z waved Havens forward. "Up here."

"I'm good, thanks." His voice was ragged, like a car knocking through its low end of gears. He looked older. In his thirties, even.

"Fine. Sit where you want." Z poked at the mass of papers piled up around her. From underneath a legal pad she pulled out what looked like a Big Mac and unwrapped it. She took a bite, then found a Coke with a straw and sipped.

"So, can someone tell me what we're here for?" Z took another bite and watched us as she chewed.

"We're here to work on wrongful convictions." Sarah Gold tapped a pen lightly against the table as she spoke. "Men who've been sentenced to death for crimes they didn't commit."

"You mean murder, Ms. Gold."

"Yes, ma'am."

"Z."

"Yes, Z."

"And what if, heaven forbid, the son of a bitch is guilty?" A pickle dropped out of Z's Big Mac. She ignored it. "What if you spend the quarter working a file and, at the end of the day, he raped the little girl, cut her into pieces, and stuffed them all into Hefty bags. Just like the state said he did."

Sarah opened her mouth to speak.

"I'm not finished," Z said. "What if you work a case and are convinced the poor bastard is innocent? Not a doubt about it. But you don't have the evidence. Or you do have the evidence, but for some reason it's tainted. Inadmissible. What then?"

Z took another bite of her sandwich, put it down, and held up her hands like she was a doctor getting ready to operate. "I'm not supposed to eat this stuff, but I love it." She wiped her fingers with a napkin, wrapped up what was left of the burger, and stuffed it into its paper bag. "My point is this. We have a lot of files. And a lot of possible outcomes. But we don't root for one result over the other."

"What do we root for?" Sarah said.

"The truth, if we can find it. And a good story. As for the actual workings of our legal system"—a flick of hands to the heavens—"sometimes it's necessary to let things fall where they may. Do you understand what I'm getting at?"

We all nodded.

"Like hell you do. But that's all right. Just keep in mind rule number one. The evidence is what it is. Allow it to tell its own story. Don't shape it to support a certain outcome. We'll talk.more about all of this later. For now, why don't we get started?" Z gestured to the stack of brown files climbing the wall behind her. "These are just a few cases you can look at. We have another roomful down the hall."

"Do we start anywhere in particular?" I said. "Or just dig in?"

"This seminar is all about instinct, Mr. Joyce. And who has it. In fact, our very first case relied on little more than a hunch. Have any of you heard this?"

We all shook our heads. Z seemed pleased.

"Our first case involved a man named Charles Granger. He was convicted of shooting a man dead over a drug deal and sentenced to die by the state of Indiana. In the spring of 1999, we read through the file in this very classroom. None of us bought it. No one was sure why, but the facts just didn't hang together. So we ordered up Granger's trial transcripts and began to work the case. We eventually zeroed in on the state's eyewitness. At first, she was scared to talk to us. We sent her some letters from Granger. Then we sent her a calendar with Granger's scheduled execution date circled. She wound up recanting her testimony, and the whole thing came apart. Charles Granger spent fifteen years on death row. At one point, he was forty-eight hours from being killed. And we saved his life. This seminar has saved eight other lives since then. And gotten at least that many released from decades of prison time for crimes they didn't commit. This will be the best work you'll ever do. It will also be the most demanding. And a lot of it will depend on you trusting your gut."

Z rattled the ice in her Coke and sucked on the straw until she hit bottom. Then she threw the cup in the vicinity of a barrel. "You've been chosen for this seminar because you're the best. At least that's what they tell me. I've won three Pulitzer Prizes in my career, so I know talent. And from where I sit, the screening committee for this course gets it right a little more than half the time. Which means at least one of you doesn't belong. But we'll see. Now, I'd like to head down the hall for a walk-through of our filing system."

Z stood. Sarah and I got up with her.

"I've already got a case." Jake Havens was still slouched in his chair, eyes fastened on the floor. "Name's James Harrison. Fourteen years ago, he was convicted of killing a ten-year-old kid in Chicago."

Z smiled so I could see her eyeteeth. "Mr. Havens. Nice of you to check in. We tend not to focus as much on cases in Illinois since the state abolished its death penalty."

Havens looked up. "What happened to 'trusting your instinct'?"

"I didn't say we couldn't take a look at an Illinois case. Just that, all things being equal, it might not be a priority."

"But all things aren't equal."

"I'm not following you."

"First of all, Harrison's dead. Fourteen months in prison and they found him stuck in the neck with a shank." Havens climbed to his feet and moved down the aisle until he stood on the other side of Sarah. He pulled a thick file from a tattered backpack and thunked it down in front of him. "This is everything I could find. Mostly newspaper clippings. And the original police report."

Z ignored the paperwork. "Why would we look into a case where the convicted man is deceased?"

"Does the fact that he's dead make him any less innocent?"

Z licked her lips. First day and the prof was pissed. Great.

"Mr. Havens, let's take this up after class . . ."

Havens pulled a wrinkled gray envelope out of his pack and laid it beside the file.

"You have something else for us?" Z's voice rose with her eyebrows.

"It's a letter, ma'am."

"I can see that."

"I received it four days ago."

"In the mail?"

"There's no stamp," Sarah said, tilting her head to get a closer look.

"It was tucked under the front door of my apartment."

"When, Mr. Havens?"

"I told you. Four days ago."

Z nodded. "Go ahead."

I could feel the shift in the room. Z was no longer the teacher. And Jake Havens, no longer just a student.

"I woke up and it was sitting in my hallway. So I opened it."

"Who else has handled it?"

"No one."

"You're sure?"

"Pretty sure."

"And what do you think is in there?"

"I know what's in there. It's a note from the killer. The real killer."

Z walked to the back of the classroom and closed the door. She returned with a box of latex gloves. We each took a pair and snapped them on. I couldn't take my eyes off the envelope. Z's cloak-and-dagger only made things better. She picked up the envelope and studied it. There was no address, just JAKE HAVENS printed in block letters of black ink.

"Was it sealed, Mr. Havens?"

Jake shook his head. Z didn't seem surprised. She opened the envelope and eased out its contents—a single sheet of paper filled with more block lettering. Z pressed the page flat on the table and we all read.

98-2425 . . . I KILT THE BOY.

"There's something else." Havens reached into his pack again, this time pulling out a small piece of cloth. He placed it down beside the letter. My hand picked it up before the rest of me realized what I'd done. It was a ragged cut. The fabric, white with a black stripe running through it.

"Looks like it's from a shirt," I said.

"It was in with the note," Havens said. "I think it's got blood on it."

Sarah had taken the piece of cloth from me. Now, she let it slip from her fingers.

"My guess," Havens continued, "is that it was cut from the shirt the victim was wearing."

"How do you know what the victim was wearing?" Z said.

Havens placed a hand on the file. "Case number 98-2425. The victim's name was Skylar Wingate. According to the cops, he was wearing a black-and-white cotton shirt. Seems to match what we've got here."

Z sighed like she'd heard it all before. "You're leaving out a few facts, Mr. Havens."

"You remember the case?" I said.

"It was a pretty big deal in its day."

"What did he leave out?" Sarah said.

"As I recall," Z said, "they did DNA testing on blood found on the jeans James Harrison was wearing when he was arrested. Came back as a perfect match to the victim."

Sarah and I turned our gaze back to Havens.

"The DNA testing was done postconviction," Havens said. "Harrison demanded and paid for it himself."

"What does that matter?" Sarah said.

"Why does a guy who's filing an appeal pay for DNA testing that's going to remove all doubt of his guilt?" Havens said.

"Desperation," Z said. "Do enough of these stories, and you'll learn all about it."

I picked up the piece of torn fabric. "Would they still have the shirt in evidence?"

"If this guy was killed in prison," Sarah said, "why would they keep anything?"

We all turned again to Z, who seemed to think long and hard for a moment. She scribbled something on a legal pad and pushed it over to Havens. "The Cook County Clerk's Office takes custody of trial transcripts and physical evidence once a case is closed. Transcripts and related trial documents are stored off-site, in a permanent records center. Actual physical evidence is kept in the county's warehouse. I've given you both addresses and a couple of names. I doubt there's anything left, but if there is, they'll have it."

"Will they let us in?" Havens said. "I mean if we just tell them we're from Medill?"

"Not likely. I'll make a call this afternoon and e-mail you if I get an okay. Assuming I do, you guys go down there and see what you can dig up on the shirt. Show me something substantive next time we meet, something that gives us a way around the DNA match . . . or we move on. Fair enough?"

We looked at one another and nodded. Z tucked the torn piece of shirt into the gray envelope and pinched it between her fingers. "Meanwhile, this stays with me. Now, does anyone else have anything they want to share? A Christmas card from John Wayne Gacy? Richard Speck's bra and panties? No? Good. If it's all right with Mr. Havens, I'd appreciate ten minutes of your precious time to talk about the five hundred or so other cases we're working here at Medill."

2

I ordered a pint of Harp, took a sip, and exhaled. All in all, the first class hadn't been too bad. Z seemed a little whacked. And then there was Havens and the letter. But that was for another day. Right now, I was sitting in Tommy Nevin's, Evanston's best Irish pub, sipping a beer, munching from a bag of Tayto crisps, and waiting for Sarah Gold to return from the bathroom.

"Sorry." She slid into her seat and smiled. "How did you know I drink Guinness?"

I shrugged. How did I know she drank Guinness? The same way I knew she liked her fries salted with vinegar and three miniburgers instead of one big cheeseburger. The same way I knew she took four early morning classes during the first quarter of her senior year. The same way I knew her favorite jeans were a ripped pair of Levi's she wore with an old checked shirt. The same way I knew she used Ivory soap, wore her hair up off her neck on Fridays, and liked to sit under an umbrella sometimes and watch the rain fall. I knew more about Sarah Gold than I knew about myself. In the end, maybe that wasn't saying very much. But there it was.

"Took a guess," I said.

Sarah sipped from her pint. There was a silky line of froth on her lip. I gestured to my own face.

"Sign of a good pint," she said and wiped her mouth with the back of her hand. "I didn't see you around much in undergrad."

"I was away a lot."

"Away?"

"I studied abroad for a year." I hadn't gone any farther than the library to study during my four years at Northwestern, but I wasn't going to tell Sarah Gold that. Besides, I kind of liked the man of mystery thing.

"Really. Where did you study?"

"Turkey." Turkey. Where did that come from? I tried to think of what I knew about the city. Until I realized it was a country. Then all I could think of was Thanksgiving. Jesus. I took a breath.

"That's exciting," Sarah said. "I spent a couple of months in Istanbul."

I smiled thickly and drained what was left of my pint. She'd barely dented hers. I put my hand up for the waitress who took my order. Sarah just shook her head and the waitress left.

"What did you think of today?" she said.

I didn't know what to think about today. Not that Sarah was waiting for an answer.

"I thought it was a little odd," she said. "I mean just turning us loose on the files. But I heard that's how Zombrowski is. Real sink-or-swim type of stuff."

We were sitting in a booth by a set of windows that looked out over Sherman Avenue. I had my back to the bar and could hear a low, pleasant chatter behind me. A floorboard creaked, and there was suddenly someone at my shoulder. Sarah's eyes widened, and she ventured a cautious smile.

"Hey, Kyle."

Kyle Brennan was a year behind us at Northwestern and a starting cornerback on the football team. I'd hated him for two years. The same two years he'd dated Sarah Gold. She'd dumped him a few months before she graduated. I thought it was a great move. From what I heard, Brennan didn't agree.

"Hey." Brennan was maybe six two, with dark eyes, short black hair, and, best I could tell, purple lips. He slid into the booth beside his ex. Essentially, right on top of her. Sarah gave herself a little space and gestured toward me.

"Kyle, do you know Ian Joyce?"

Brennan shook his head without looking at me and took a sip from a large plastic cup. Summer practice started next week, and a lot of the football types were getting their drink on while they could. Brennan appeared to be leading the charge.

"Ian graduated with me," Sarah said. "We're in a seminar together."

"Some of us are headed into the city," Brennan said. "Street festival in Wrigleyville. Why don't you come?"

"No thanks, Kyle."

"We can hang out."

"No thanks."

"I said we can hang."

I leaned across. "And she said, 'No thanks.'"

Brennan slammed his hand on the table and spilled some of his drink. It was purple, which explained the lips.

"Who the fuck was talking to you?"

The buzz around us grew quiet. I could feel the tension ripple across the room and tried to play it off.

"Relax, pal. I'm thinking you're about thirty seconds from getting tossed out of here."

"I'm not your pal. And do you think I give a fuck?"

I gripped the edge of the table and felt the flush up into the roots of my hair.

"Kyle." Sarah grabbed her ex by the arm. "Look at me."

He did.

"You're drunk. And you're embarrassing me. Leave now and I'll call you tomorrow. We'll grab some lunch." She touched the side of his face and gave him a quick kiss. I almost threw up. But Brennan left.

"Asshole," Sarah said, and waved as Brennan walked out of Nevin's with two of his pals.

"You gonna call him?"

"He won't even remember talking to me. I just wanted to make sure he didn't tear the place apart."

"You don't think I could have handled him?"

Sarah looked at me—all six feet, hundred seventy pounds—and shook her head. "He'd kill you."

"You're probably right."

Sarah lifted her pint. "Enough of that. What were we talking about?"

"The seminar."

"Oh, yeah. Tell me this. What do you think of our classmate?"

"Havens?"

"You know anything about him?" Sarah spoke like she knew a lot and was waiting to unload.

"I heard he went to the University of Chicago."

"Law school. Top of the class. Editor in chief of the *Law Review*."

"So what's he doing here?"

Northwestern's Medill School of Journalism was probably the best in the world. Or at least in the top two. Still, it was journalism. The average pay coming out of Medill was thirty to fifty K a year. And that's if you landed in a big market. Editor in chief of the *Law Review* at Chicago could easily triple that. I knew the numbers. Mostly because I'd managed a nearly perfect score on my LSAT. So I'd thought it through.

"Havens doesn't want to be a lawyer," Sarah said. "Just did it for kicks."

"Number one at U of C Law School . . . for kicks?"

"Actually, there's more to it than that. He got involved during his third year with a legal aid clinic on the South Side. Worked on a child abuse case. From what I hear he freaked out some people with his intensity."

"I could see that."

"Yeah, well, I guess he decided the law wasn't his thing."

"And what does the boy genius want now?"

"No one knows. Except he wanted into Medill, and specifically this seminar."

"How do you know that?"

"I do my homework, Ian. Havens actually negotiated his admission into Medill. Told the school he'd enroll, but only if he was guaranteed a seat in Z's seminar."

"And Medill went for it?"

"Why not? Big-time student. And they were probably going to let him into the class anyway."

The talk about Havens was interesting. So much so that I'd forgotten whom I was talking to. Now I caught a whiff of her from across the table. She wore a thin gold chain around her neck. A vein beat softly in the hollow of her throat.

"What do you think?" Sarah said.

"About what?"

"Havens?"

"Oh, yeah. He wanted in on the seminar. So what?"

"That letter he found was pretty strange."

"It's probably nothing."

"Probably." Sarah took a small sip from her pint. "Can I tell you something else?"

"Sure."

"I don't belong in this class."

"What are you talking about?"

"Everyone at school knows how smart you are, Ian. And, no offense, Havens might be even smarter. I'm out of my league."

"Bullshit. You applied and got in. You belong."

She lifted her chin a fraction. "You know *why* I got in?"

"I'm not sure why *I* got in."

"Please. The only reason I got in was because of my work with Omega."

"Omega?"

"It's a women's organization in Evanston. They run a shelter service for abused women. We set up safe houses and move women in and out of them. Hide them from the assholes trying to beat them up until they can make other arrangements."

"And you work there?"

"I volunteer. One night we were taking a woman out of her house and the husband showed up drunk. Bashed in my windshield with a baseball bat."

"Did you get her out?"

"You bet. I wrote a couple of articles about it for one of my classes."

"Holy shit. I'd like to read them."

Sarah touched my hand, and I felt my heart jump. "Thanks, Ian. I'll show them to you. Anyway, that's why I got into this seminar. My teacher loved the stories and pushed for me. Actually, it's kind of ironic now that I think about it."

"What's that?"

"Me trying to help abused women and hooking up with a jerk like Kyle."

"You can't quit, Sarah. Not after one class."

"Who said anything about quitting?"

"You just told me you weren't good enough."

"Oh. I was just venting. I'm plenty good."

"So you're not gonna quit?"

"And let Jake Havens get the last laugh. Please." She tipped her eyes toward the front door. "Speak of the devil."

I turned and looked. Jake Havens had slipped onto a stool and ordered himself a drink.

Havens was staring at a line of bottles behind the bar. Light glinted off the glass. I tapped him on the shoulder. It was a workingman's shoulder, full of knotted muscle, tendon, and sinew. Havens turned a fraction.

"What's up?"

"Thought you might like to come over for a drink?"

Havens nodded to the booth and Sarah, alone in it. "You two pals?" Up close his features were hard and clean, betraying no real interest in the question he'd just asked or whatever response might come back.

"We went to undergrad together," I said.

"I figured that." Havens picked up his pint and led the way back to Sarah. Like it was his idea and I could come along if I wanted.

"Sarah Gold. Like the name." He slid into the booth and immediately owned it. I pulled up a chair. It was almost five now, and Nevin's was filling with an after-class, happy-hour vibe. Everything seemed to dim, however, as Havens leaned across the table.

"That your boyfriend who was in here?"

"My ex."

"You got a lot of ghosts following you around?"

"Excuse me?"

"Forget it." Havens took a sip of his beer. "What did you think of today?"

"Honestly?" Sarah said. "I thought there'd be more guidance."

"You mean hand-holding?"

She threw Havens's condescension back at him with a smirk of her own. He'd have to do a lot better if he wanted to get under Sarah's skin. Or anywhere else, for that matter.

"I'd think she might want to set up some parameters for our research," Sarah said. "Maybe an overview. A little more background on cases she'd like us to look at. A section of the country to focus on."

"I already have a case."

"So you told us." Sarah's eyes brushed mine, then danced away.

"Why don't you take a look?" Havens pulled his backpack onto the table.

"Actually, I've got to get going." Sarah was on her feet, looking down at Havens, making him seem suddenly small. And being infuriatingly nice about it. Inside, I was tickled. Havens took it in stride.

"Z just e-mailed me. She got the okay from the clerk's office for tomorrow. It's a Saturday, but I guess the county people are there in the morning. You guys have cars?"

We both nodded. Sarah slumped into the booth. Havens was back in control.

"Here's what I'm thinking," he said. "One of us takes the records center. Goes through all the paper files on Harrison and pulls out whatever's relevant. The other two go to the evidence warehouse. See what's there."

"I'll take the records center," Sarah said.

I looked over at her. "Evidence warehouse sounds like more fun."

"Picking through the bloody clothes of a dead little boy? No thanks."

Havens shrugged. "Fine with me. I'll e-mail the addresses to both of you. They open at nine. Z suggested we get there first thing. Joyce, why don't I meet you there . . ."

Sarah's head snapped to one side as Kyle Brennan slammed back into the booth beside her. He had both elbows on the table and his nose pressed close to her cheek. "Miss me?"

Sarah looked more embarrassed than alarmed and pushed at her ex's forearm. He crowded in closer.

"Fuck these losers. Let's get out of here. Head into the city." Brennan put a hand on her shoulder. His other went under the table.

"Kyle, no."

"Hey, asshole." I made a move toward Brennan, not really sure what I hoped to accomplish once I got there. Fortunately, Havens beat me to it.

He dragged Brennan out of the booth and put him on his belly. It took all of three seconds. Brennan flopped like a fish at the bottom of a boat. Havens kept a knee in his spine and a forearm across the back of his neck. "You need to calm down." Havens cinched his knee down a touch so the side of Brennan's face pressed flat against the sticky barroom floor. There was a low hissing sound. That was Brennan, struggling to breathe.

"Hey, man. Let him up." One of Brennan buddies stepped forward, but not too far.

"He's fine," Havens said. "Just taking a little time-out."

Brennan grunted and flipped onto his side, swinging an elbow in the general direction of Havens's jaw. Havens leaned back and looped one arm around Brennan's neck, his Adam's apple fixed firmly in the crook of Havens's elbow. Havens flexed. Brennan's eyes fluttered, then closed. His chest didn't look like it was moving. The already quiet bar had turned into a morgue.

"Let him up," I said. Havens glanced at me, then released his grip. Brennan's pals rushed in. The football player hung limp in their arms.

"Sit him up straight," Havens said. They did. Havens punched Brennan once in the back, between the shoulder blades. He coughed and his eyes flickered open.

"Get him out of here," Havens said. No one had to be told twice. Havens slid back into the booth. I looked around for Sarah.

"She left," Havens said. "Probably too embarrassed."

I took a seat across from him. We were quiet for another minute.

"Where did you learn all that?" I said.

"All what?"

"Putting a guy out like that?"

Havens shrugged. There was a long scratch and fresh blood on his forearm, but he didn't seem to notice.

"You lift weights?" I said.

"I used to long line tuna out of Chatham and Gloucester."

"New England?"

"I fished full-time for three years. Worked Georges Banks a week, month, at a time. Slept on the boat. Snow, ice. All kinds of seas. Hauling heavy lines and nets." Havens moved his hands to cup his pint. "Don't need weights when you're doing that."

"Huh."

We fell silent again. I could hear some talk at the bar, but everyone seemed to be giving us a wide berth. Havens began to pull papers out of his backpack. "You want to take a look at what I've got on the case?"

"Why not?"

He nodded like that was the only sensible answer. "I heard you're one of the stars up here."

"Up where?" I said.

Havens raised his chin. "Here."

"I don't have time for that stuff."

"What stuff?"

"The Chicago-Northwestern stuff. Our school's better. More rigorous. Academically pure. All that garbage."

"You think that's what goes on in Hyde Park?"

"It goes on in Evanston. And it's what I'm hearing from you. Listen, I know you're a smart guy. Now, I know you're a badass, too. Good for you. Great for you. I probably couldn't beat myself up. But I'm smart. Never been a problem. Sarah's no dummy either."

"You sure about that?"

"Positive. So why don't we cut the bullshit and work together. You're a goddamn lawyer on top of everything else. Let's just get into the cases. Your case, Z's case, any case. Pick one out and see what we can dig up."

"Is Gold okay with that?" Havens said.

"I don't know Sarah that well, but I think she's a pretty straight shooter."

"What does that mean?"

"Fucked if I know. Just thought it sounded good."

Havens cracked a smile that seemed genuine enough and lifted his mostly empty glass. "You got a thing for her."

"Hardly."

"Been like that since when? Sophomore year?"

"Fuck you."

Havens widened his eyes and opened his mouth to laugh. His teeth, of course, were white and straight. "Jesus Christ, Joyce. Lighten up."

Jake Havens could kick the shit out of me in any one of a half-dozen ways, but I didn't care. I never cared. And that had gotten me a nice ass kicking more times than I cared to count.

"Can't blame you," he continued. "We all got one, right? Maybe more than one. Besides, she's pretty hot."

"Yeah, Sarah's hot."

"But it's her world and you're just in it?"

"Something like that."

"'Something like that.' Exactly like that. Welcome to the club, my friend. I'm gonna get another one. You?"

"Thanks."

Havens headed to the bar.

"Hey," I said.

Havens turned, empty pint glasses in both hands.

"You really think Harrison's innocent?"

Havens slipped back into the booth. "Forget the letter. You saw the shirt. If that's from the victim, it should be easy to prove. And if it *is* real . . ."

"Then it was sent by the killer."

"Not necessarily."

I tilted my head and frowned. "That's what you told Z."

"But that's not the only possibility, is it? If that shirt was part of the state's evidence, anyone with access could have sent me a piece. Cop, prosecutor, evidence tech."

"A whistle-blower?"

"Could be. Someone sending us a message. Telling us this guy was framed."

"Is that what you think?"

"I don't think anything . . . until we see the evidence."

"But why send the letter to you? Why not the *Trib*? *Sun-Times*? I mean, you're a student in a seminar."

"You don't think I've been wondering that myself? Read the file."

Havens went to get our drinks. I picked through newspaper clippings from the murder. At the bottom of the pile, I found the original police report filed on Skylar Wingate's disappearance. Clipped to the back was a photo from the crime scene. A shallow hole in the ground, a small white body bag beside it. I ran a finger over the picture. Then I put it aside and began to read.

3

Skylar Wingate was last seen alive by his older brother, Bobby. He told police Skylar left St. Augustine Elementary School on the city's Northwest Side around 3:45 p.m., and walked south on Lemont Avenue. Skylar was headed home, less than a mile away. Skylar's mom thought her youngest was with his older brother all afternoon and didn't become concerned until Bobby showed up, alone, at a little after six. Fifty of Chicago's finest went door-to-door, searching the white-bread neighborhood on foot until well past midnight. Skylar was described as four foot two, weighing sixty-three pounds, wearing gray pants and a black-and-white-striped shirt. Havens had underlined the last fact with a pen.

Detectives questioned Skylar's family and friends in the first few hours of the disappearance and came up with nothing. According to the *Trib,* it was three days later that a hiker found Skylar's remains in the Cook County forest preserve a mile away. Animals had dug up the body. A preliminary autopsy showed the boy had been stabbed repeatedly, strangled, and drowned before he went in the ground. I stopped reading as Havens came back with a fresh round.

"Well?" he said.

"I skimmed the police report and a couple of articles."

"You see the detail on the shirt?"

I nodded.

"This case was big at the time," Havens said. "You remember it?"

"I was eight."

"Doesn't matter. White kid, Catholic school, nice neighborhood. A lot of pressure to make an arrest." Havens glanced out the window and checked his watch. "Shit, I gotta run."

"We just got our drinks."

Havens drained half his pint in one go, gathered up his research, and stood. "See you tomorrow, Joyce. Do yourself a favor and forget about Gold. Make life a lot simpler for all of us."

I watched him walk out the door and down Sherman. The bar was packed now, and a gaggle of women hovered close by, ready to pounce on the booth once I'd vacated. I took a sip of my beer, but my heart wasn't in it. I smiled at the women as I got up and presented them with their prize. One of them even smiled back. The other three pushed past, calling for the waitress and settling in. I wandered out of Nevin's and squinted against a harsh, slanting light. It was just past six, still a couple of hours before darkness dropped over Lake Michigan. I walked down the street, thinking about Jake Havens. A horn beeped once from under an overpass. Sarah Gold sat in the front seat of a black Audi. She hustled me over with a wave of her hand.

"Get in," she said. I did so without a word.

"Put your head down," she said and scrunched low in her seat. I did the same and heard a car cruise past. Sarah popped up and turned over the engine.

"What are we doing?" I said.

"Following him." Sarah swung into traffic.

"Following who?"

She pointed to a silver Honda, three cars ahead of us. "Havens."

"Why?" The plan struck me as wonderful, although I had no real idea why.

"He's up to something," Sarah said. "And he's holding all the cards."

"What cards?"

"Everything. He doles out information to us as he sees fit. Heck, he was ordering Zombrowski around today."

"And we're going to get what out of this?"

"The upper hand." A smirk curled the corner of Sarah's mouth.

"What's so funny?"

"Nothing." She swung a right onto Dempster Street. "You don't think it's a good idea to be following him?"

"I think it's a fine idea."

"You're being sarcastic."

"Actually, I'm not."

"He doesn't interest you at all?"

"Not the way he interests you."

"What does that mean?"

"Nothing."

She glanced across the car. "Sounded like something."

I pointed at the flow of traffic ahead of us. "Where do you think he's going?"

"Tell me what you meant."

"When?"

"Just now."

"He likes you, Sarah."

"That's what you think?"

"Yes, that's what I think. Watch where you're going."

She moved her eyes back to the road. "He doesn't like me. And he's not my type anyway."

"Maybe you're just pissed because he beat up your boyfriend?"

"Kyle's not my boyfriend. And he got what was coming to him."

We drove a couple more blocks in silence. I didn't know what else to say. Havens had a thing for Sarah. And no one was going to convince me otherwise. I mean, why the hell wouldn't he? Why wouldn't anyone? The fact that she couldn't see it didn't mean anything. I was walking proof of that.

"What are we going to do if he catches us?" I said.

"We'll tell him the truth."

"Which is what?"

"He's creeping us out. And we want to know what's up."

"That'll go over well."

We pulled up to a light. Havens's Honda sat two cars ahead. I wondered if Sarah had ever tailed anyone before. All in all, I thought she was doing a pretty good job. We took a left on McCormick Boulevard, before turning west on Devon.

"He's headed to the forest preserve," I said.

"The what?"

"The woods. He's headed to the woods where they buried the kid."

Sarah hadn't taken a look at the police report, at least not enough to put it together. So I did it for her.

"Skylar Wingate. The kid James Harrison killed. They found him down here."

A sign flashed past: CALDWELL WOODS. Up ahead, Havens's blinker blinked.

"He's going in a side entrance," I said. "I think there's a small parking lot there."

"What should we do?"

"Take a right." We pulled into a warren of residential streets and parked.

"Come on," I said, "before we lose him."

We jogged back across Caldwell Avenue and stopped just inside the entrance to the forest preserve. I heard a car door slam and waited another beat. Then we slipped forward. Havens was just making his way down one of the trails. We followed.

4

Sunlight washed down the dirt path and cut a filtered edge through the trees. Sarah had a bounce in her step. I didn't.

"What should we say if he sees us?" she said.

"I told you. I don't know. This whole thing was your idea."

Havens had slipped around a bend in the trail, maybe thirty yards ahead.

"Do you think he's taking us to the crime scene?" she said.

"Be a good bet. We should probably get off the trail." I found a gap in the trees and stepped into the shade. It had rained the night before and the ground here was still damp. The fecund smell of soil mingled with rotting wood and the faint metallic tang of the river.

"You've been here before?" Sarah was pressed up close behind me, and I could feel the swell of her blouse, firm against my skin.

"Yeah, I've been here."

"Why?"

"Good running trails. Sometimes, I take my bike down here. Now stay close and be quiet." I moved quickly through the trees, my eyes adjusting to the thickening darkness. Sarah struggled to keep pace. I went in about a hundred yards and waited.

"Sorry," she said, when she finally caught up. "I think I'm running into every thornbush in the place."

I nodded to a faint line of light on our left. "If I have my geography right, the path is just over there, close to the river."

"And the crime scene?"

"I figure he's taking us to the grave."

The word sucked the life from the air between us and drained the color from Sarah's face. She was a child again, staring up at me out of her own dark hole of fear.

"It's all right," I said. "He's not going to know we're around. And if he does, big deal."

"You should lead the way."

We pushed on. Twenty yards later, I stopped. There was a scratching up ahead. Sarah couldn't hear it, but I could and pointed.

"Someone's in the trees. I'm gonna check it out. You circle back and find the trail. Walk down it until you see me."

Sarah seemed happy with the plan, especially the part that got her back on the walking path. After she'd gone, I sat up against a tree and slowed my breathing. The scratching was still there, low, insistent. Someone digging maybe. I let myself soften. Melt. When I was loose and limber, I eased to my feet. The ground was sloping away from me. I picked a path through the tangle of underbrush. Not a scrape of sound. I'd always been pretty good moving through the woods. Even as a kid. I didn't know why, but everyone was good at something.

I could see a glimmer of light and stopped again to listen. The scratching wasn't there anymore. The digging had stopped as well. Nothing now but crickets. There was a sudden thrashing in the trees to my left. A grunt, and then a scream. A woman's scream. Sarah's scream.

5

A twist of thorns whipped across my face, drawing fresh blood I could feel on my cheek and taste on my lips. I pushed through the thicket and heard the scream again. I weaved between the dark trunks of trees, keeping my legs high so I didn't get caught in the tangle. Suddenly, the ground dropped away completely. I caught myself and navigated a small, steep incline, stepping out of the tree line onto a hard-packed trail. The smell of the river was strong now, but it was dark enough that I couldn't see the water. I could see Sarah, however. She lay a few feet from me. Jake Havens stood over her. He had a knife in his hand.

"Easy," I said.

Havens flashed the knife, then clicked it shut and slipped it into a pocket. His movements were quick and sure, designed for places like the deep of the Cook County forest preserve. He reached down and touched two fingers to Sarah's throat. I noticed for the first time that her eyes were closed. There was a small egg rising under the thin skin near her temple. Havens lifted her off the path and carried her to a patch of grass. He disappeared and returned with a bandana, soaked in cold water. He bathed her face and wrapped it around her neck.

"She fell down the embankment." Havens kept his back to me and pointed to the drop-off. I guess I could have picked up a rock and hit him. He didn't seem too worried about it.

"Is she all right?" I said.

"Pulse is strong. Give her a minute." Havens turned, his features cut fine by the final shards of the day's light. "You're bleeding, Joyce."

"Thornbush." I wiped my face with the back of my hand. Sarah moaned lightly and began to stir.

"How you feeling?" There was a tenderness in Havens's voice that surprised me. Sarah smiled at the sound, and my surprise blossomed into jealousy.

"Hey, Sarah. You okay?" I moved closer and knelt down beside her.

"I'm fine. Just a little dizzy."

Havens produced a flashlight and checked her eyes. "Pupils are constricting. Can you stand up?"

He helped her to her feet.

"I'm fine." Sarah felt the lump on her head. "Bet that looks great."

Havens smiled. "You wear it well, Gold."

"Thanks." She took his bandana off, wrung it out, and held it against her cheek.

I grabbed Havens by the sleeve and turned him around. "You want to tell us what we're doing out here?"

Havens threw a hand to his left. "The Chicago River is fifteen feet that way."

"So?" I said.

"So that's where he killed him."

"Who?" Sarah said.

Havens stepped a little closer. "Who do you think? Skylar Wingate."

Havens took us to the grave, nothing left to mark it but a small, dark depression in the ground. Still, in the failing light, I could see it all. The boy's body, coming up and out of the water, glistening and wet, then cold and hard as it dried on the riverbank. Heels digging twin furrows in the mud as he was dragged to the place. He lay there, mouth open, limbs tangled, one palm half closed as the hole was dug . . . or maybe just some last-minute depth added to it. Then down he went. A soft thump when he hit bottom. And the dirt went in, over his face first because of the eyes. After that the rest, covered over with soil, wet and heavy, alive with the woods. I could hear him now, fists beating against the soft cover. Felt him, too, up and down the back of my neck. Stiff fingers. Cold, pimpled flesh. I looked over at Sarah and saw the little girl again. Only this time, she screamed without making a sound.

"He's gone," I said.

"I know."

I took her hand in mine and tried to coax some warmth into it. Havens had wandered back down to the river. Left us alone to wake a boy we never knew. Now Havens's voice beckoned through the screen of trees. We turned from the grave. Skylar Wingate's memory floated and followed.

6

Havens was perched on a large boulder, jutting up like an angry tooth out of the riverbank. Sarah and I found spots on the grass at his feet. Just the way he liked it, I thought.

"Police think he was pulled out of the water right here." Havens pointed to the river behind him. The night was almost full now; the water rippled under fresh strokes of moonlight.

"That was fourteen years ago," I said. "I still don't understand why you're down here."

"Big picture, Joyce."

"What does that mean?" Sarah said.

"There was something I didn't tell Z. A fresh case. Less than a week ago."

Sarah struggled to her feet. I motioned for her to sit.

"Where?" I said.

"A kid went missing on the North Side. They found a sneaker and what they believe to be his backpack maybe a mile along this trail."

"No body?"

"They searched for three days and came up with nothing. The kid was a runaway so it wasn't a big story. Anyway, it was close to Wingate and I wanted to take a look."

"It's an active crime scene," Sarah said. "You can't just go barging in."

"Chicago PD finished up last week. The site's been fully processed for evidence." Havens climbed down off his rock and began to walk. Sarah and I followed.

"The boy's belongings were found in a small clearing, at the foot of some rocks." Havens took out his flashlight and began to play it along the riverbank.

"And you think you'll know the place when you see it?" I said. "In the middle of the night?"

"I was hoping to get here earlier, but I got held up by some class-mates." Havens turned. "Seems they got lost in the woods. Come on. I got a feeling it's just up ahead."

Havens never found the scene. Sarah did. Or rather, she found a scrap of police tape flapping yellow in the night. Sarah pulled it off the branch of a tree and showed it to Havens. "This what you're looking for?"

Havens stuffed the tape into his pocket and pushed deeper into the woods. Sarah held her hand high and I slapped her five as I went by. It took another ten minutes of fumbling before we broke into the actual clearing, bordered by a dark outcropping of rocks on one side and the river on the other. I edged ahead of the group and drifted toward the water. Havens warned me to be careful. He was right. I took a false step and felt the bank give way. My footing went and I was suddenly underwater, breathing in black mud. I came up blow-ing gusts from my mouth and nose. Havens's light bobbled in the darkness. I grabbed for it. There was a hand there. It gripped my fore-arm and pulled. The mud gave a sucking sound, unwilling to give up its prize. But Havens wouldn't be denied. Sarah watched without mercy as I was saved from myself and laid out on the bank. Cold, wet, and humiliated. So much for being good in the woods.

"Sorry," I gasped.

"It happens," Havens said and dismissed my fall with a shrug. For the first time I felt a tingling of "like" for my classmate.

"You need a minute?" he said.

I shook my head and got to my feet. Carvings of mud fell off my pants and shoes.

"This has to be where they found the pack," Havens said, eyes fixed on mine. I took the flashlight from him. My jeans and boots squeaked and squelched as I moved. Something was crawling down my neck. I knocked it away with the back of my hand and crouched to study the terrain.

"What are you looking for?" Sarah crouched beside me.

"I don't know." I dug at the dirt. My fingers went in less than an inch. "Soil's thin. If he killed the boy here, he couldn't have buried him." I flicked the light up into the tree line. "I guess he could have dragged him into the woods."

"But he didn't." Sarah trickled a stream of pebbles through her fingers. "The police already checked."

"Why did they stop searching?" I said, turning the light in Havens's direction.

"According to the *Herald,* the cops now believe the kid might have just left the area," he said. "They're pursuing 'other leads,' whatever that means."

I got up and began to walk along the riverbank. Carefully this time.

"Where are you going?" Sarah's voice crept quietly beside me.

"There might be a place . . ." I tracked the curve of the river. After about thirty yards, I cut away from the water and climbed partway up a slope of crumbling granite. I touched a finger to my lips. A ruffle of breeze tickled the tops of the trees and licked at the water's edge.

"He took the boy off the street?" My voice hovered just above a hush.

"That was the theory," Havens said.

I peered up the slope. "He still might need a place."

"A place for what?" Sarah said.

I looked back at her. "To be alone with the body."

I turned to climb again. Havens followed. Sarah came last.

7

It was Havens who found it. A small cleft in a wall of rock, something you'd never notice in the dark, unless that's exactly what you were looking for. We stopped at the mouth of the cave.

"I don't like this." Sarah's voice was high and strained.

"We'll just take a quick look," Havens said.

I ran the flashlight back down the slope, toward the purring black river. To my left, I heard a crack, a step in the woods.

"Animals," Havens said.

I cut the light and listened. Another crack. Then two more.

"Relax," Havens said and grabbed the flashlight before disappearing through the opening. Sarah's face shone under the moonlight. I gestured for her to follow. Then I ducked my head and went in.

The cave was bigger than its entrance suggested. I took the flashlight back from Havens and stretched it along one wall.

"Anybody home?" Havens said.

I moved toward the back of the cave. My eye caught a glint of silver. I nudged a Coors Light beer can with my foot. Two more were crushed and tossed nearby.

"Check it out." Sarah was just inside the entrance, reaching for a garbage bag someone had cut down the side and spread out on the ground.

"Don't touch it," I said. Sarah kicked the bag aside. Underneath were fast-food wrappers, the remnants of someone's dinner.

"Looks like someone made a fire here as well," Sarah said.

"Probably used the garbage bag as a poncho or blanket," Havens said, sliding to the ground to examine her find.

I moved along a long, narrow passage, away from my friends' voices and the thin threads of light leaking in from outside. Sarah called my name once. Then I was alone. I let the light play over the walls, patterns of rock drifting and moving. I actually smelled him before I saw him.

A single eye. Cobalt blue.

Snapshot.

His body. Small. White. Naked.

Snapshot.

A gray T-shirt, torn into strips and wrapped tight around his neck. Hands and feet bound with dirty pieces of twine.

Snapshot.

Snapshot.

The boy's mouth was stretched open as if to scream. But it wasn't he who screamed. To my surprise, it was me.

8

Havens got to me first. "You okay?"

What I thought was a scream had turned out to be more like a gasp. Havens waited for me to speak, but I just looked at him. Sarah picked up the flashlight I'd dropped on the floor of the cave. That was when they both saw him.

"Holy shit." Havens moved closer. Sarah remained rooted where she stood.

"Don't touch anything," I said.

"We need to make sure he's dead." Sarah's voice seemed to grow smaller by the syllable.

"He's dead," Havens said and took a step back. "Looks like the animals have been at him."

I took Sarah's arm and guided her back down the passage. "Move out the way you came. Exactly the way you came. And don't touch anything."

We backed out of the cave and huddled by its mouth. After what we'd found inside, the air felt cool and fresh on my face.

"Think we contaminated anything?" Havens said.

I looked at Sarah. She shook her head.

"How about you, Jake?"

"Didn't touch a thing."

"Let me see your shoes," I said.

They were both wearing sneakers. Sarah, Nike. Havens, New Balance.

"Generic enough," I said. "We're probably fine."

Havens looked at me with curiosity and, maybe, a touch of respect. Off to the left, another branch popped. We fell silent, considering one another in the dense light. A creak followed, like someone was shifting his weight, settling. I gestured for Havens and Sarah to stay where they were. Then I eased into the scrub to the right of the cave. The moon was cut off on this side of the rocks, plunging the slope into a world of purples and blacks. I slipped down, this time disturbing nary a pebble, then looped to the left. Inside the tree line, I found a trail and began to work back toward the cave. Along the way, I picked up a rock, as large as my fist, smooth, and heavy. It felt good in my hand.

I came up against the slick trunk of a tree and wound my head and shoulders around it. Through a tangle, I could see the river, alive in the night. Straight ahead, the trees marched out in a checkerboard pattern. To my right, a riot of vegetation grew in a twisted mass. I let my eyes defocus and reassemble the scene. The tangle separated into bushes and branches, humpbacked roots, and, at the very center, a large, flat boulder. On the boulder sat something. Something breathing.

A pair of yellow eyes stared intently up the slope. Toward the cave. The eyes blinked once and a soft moan issued. It was an aching that pricked the back of my neck. I slipped down to my belly and crawled forward. I'd covered maybe ten feet when there was a thrashing and rolling above me. A slide of rocks rumbled down the slope, followed by the hammer of feet. Yellow eyes rose up from his perch. His silhouette turned to look at me, as if he'd known I was there all along. Then he was gone. I scrambled to my feet. Havens was somewhere nearby, whispering my name. A roar in the darkness.

"Over here," I said and fought my way out of the trees. Havens pulled me to the ground.

"There was something there," I said. "Got spooked when you came down the hill."

"Something? Human or animal?"

"Couldn't tell."

"Forget about it," Havens said. "We've got bigger problems. Definitely human problems. Come on."

9

The man with the yellow eyes ran smoothly, silently, navigating a slalom course of limbs and roots, hunks of bushes, and chunks of trees. All twisted and curved in the night. Once he'd called in the body, he knew it was dangerous to come back. And knew he couldn't resist. He loved to watch the police when they found one. Loved to watch them work. So he'd made his plans and marked out his escape. If anyone did manage to follow . . . He gripped the handle of the knife dangling from a cord around his neck. Well, he had a plan for that as well.

A half mile later, he stepped out of the tree line and into a residential cul-de-sac. His heart rate registered a blip past sixty. His walk was cat quiet. He made his way slowly down the block and thought about the encounter in the woods. He'd sensed something familiar. Something disturbing. He turned the corner at Devon Avenue. There was a Metra stop less than a mile away. As luck would have it, a train into the city was arriving just as he got there.

10

Jake Havens and I scrambled back up the slope and found Sarah, sitting a good distance from the entrance to the cave. From the top of the ridge, I could see the reason for Havens's concern. A line of flashlights snaked out from the forest preserve's main parking lot, twisting through the woods, heading straight for us. In the lot itself were four or five sets of flashing blue lights. Squad cars. I grabbed Sarah by the arm and motioned for Havens to follow. We kept low, skirting the edge of the slope for maybe fifty yards. I checked the lights again. They were closer now. I heard the pop and squelch of a police radio, then a muffled curse. Sarah gripped my hand. Havens seemed calm, perhaps a little curious to see what I had planned. The footing was firmer here, a hardpan of rock dropping away. We went down quietly and were quickly swallowed by the trees. I moved uphill, keeping Sarah's hand in mine. I didn't know if Havens was still with us, but he wasn't making any noise, and that's what mattered. We climbed for about a quarter mile until we picked up a trail. Then we broke into a light jog. Two hundred yards later, the trail ended in a small, sheltered space. From this vantage point we had a clear view of the woods. A loose necklace of lights hugged the river's edge, moving steadily in our direction. They stopped occasionally, clustering together and then spreading out again.

"What do you think they're looking for?" Havens said.

"What were we looking for?" Sarah said.

The flashlights winked as they ducked in and out of cover. For a few moments the lights disappeared altogether. Then they were back, closer now, growing larger in the night.

"They're climbing," I said. We scooted back into the tree line. The lights stopped and started, zigzagging up the slope we'd just navigated before huddling again. One light blinked out. Then another.

"They found the cave," Havens said. A third and fourth light disappeared, leaving just one outside.

"Come on," I said. "If we hustle, we can still get your car out of the auxiliary lot. Once they call in the body, everything's gonna be shut down."

"Shit," Havens said.

I nodded. "Bet your ass. This way."

We wound through the trees and back to Caldwell Avenue. Havens took off at a jog down the street. Sarah and I went to find her car. Havens kept his lights off as he tiptoed his Honda out of the parking lot. Sarah and I followed him down Devon. We'd gone less than a mile when three more squad cars and an ambulance roared up, sirens blaring, flashers scarring the night. We pulled over and watched them go past. Then we slipped out of Chicago and back into Evanston.

II

It was almost midnight by the time we hit downtown Evanston. Havens found a spot on Sherman Avenue near Emerson. Sarah pulled in behind him.

"I need to get your cell phone numbers," she said as she climbed out of the car. We exchanged numbers, then stood on the corner. I felt the dead boy in the cave, staring at the three of us.

"I should get home," I said, checking my watch.

"I'm not sure I can sleep," Sarah said.

"Me, neither," Havens said. "Nevin's for a beer? Maybe a little postgame?"

"This isn't a football game." I was surprised at the tension in my voice and chalked it up to fatigue.

"Relax."

"We found a body tonight, Havens. Do you understand that?"

"I know what we found." Havens glanced anxiously up and down the empty block.

"I could use a beer," Sarah said quietly.

I shook my head. "You guys go ahead. I'm just gonna walk home."

"How about we give you a ride?" Sarah touched my sleeve and tried to catch my eyes.

"It's not far."

"How about we walk you?"

Somehow I found myself nodding my assent. And so the three of us started walking west along Emerson.

"Weird how we found that cave," Havens said, turning to me.

"Luck, or bad luck, depending on how you look at it."

"Someone was there before us," Sarah said. "Maybe they called the police."

"Maybe," Havens said.

"Should we tell them we were there?" Sarah glanced anxiously at both of us.

"And let the cops know we were trampling around in their crime scene?" Havens snorted. "That would be the end of our careers at Medill. Real quick."

"What if the cave is related to what we're working on?" Sarah said.

"Seems unlikely," I said. "I mean Wingate happened almost fifteen years ago."

"Let the cops handle the cave," Havens grumbled. "We've got our own murder to worry about."

We were out of the downtown area now. There was a park on our left. A couple of kids played a lonely game of one-on-one on a basketball court lit up like a stage. Otherwise, everything was dark and the night had suddenly gone quiet. I lived in the house I grew up in, on a cramped side street called Astoria. The neighborhood was poor by Evanston standards, which was to say not abject poverty, just a dreary sense of never quite making the grade. Most of the homes were two-story frames, with a patch of crabgrass out front, a patio of poured cement in the back, and generations of beaten-down anger in between. I wasn't ashamed of where I lived. I just didn't want Jake Havens and Sarah Gold anywhere near it. We got to the top of Astoria and I stopped.

"Thanks, guys."

"Which one is yours?" I could feel Havens's eyes crawling down the block, opening doors to people's lives and sniffing around inside.

"Down there," I said and pointed vaguely.

"The green-and-white one?" Havens said.

"Yeah."

There was an awkward pause before Sarah leaned in to give me a hug. "Put something on those scrapes."

"Get some ice for your face. Tomorrow, Havens."

"Keep a lid on what we saw in the cave, Joyce."

"No kidding."

Havens grunted, and the two of them walked away. They made a handsome couple as they left. Young and poised, heads held high, strides in perfect sync. I waited until they turned the corner, convinced Havens would sneak back down the street. When he didn't, I walked toward my house.

The shades were drawn on the second floor. All the lights were out, save for a bloom of yellow in the living room. The front door was old and heavy. The key turned easily in the lock. Once inside, I kept my keys in one hand and walked down the long hallway of my youth. At the end was the door to the bedroom I'd shared with my brother. Beside it was a second door, with another lock. It led to the cellar.

I opened the second door and headed down. I could hear the chatter of rats in the walls as I creaked down the stairs. It was pitch-black, but my feet walked the space like it was my own coffin. I found the string and pulled. A single bulb cast pale light across the basement. I pushed at a mat of cobwebs that hung off a rafter. Black mildew and decay spotted the ceiling. There must have been a leak somewhere. There were leaks everywhere.

I sat on the stairs and looked around. Chains, heavy and tinted with rust, winked at me in the murk. Coils of rope lay at my feet. My eyes went where they always went. To a hole in the floor sealed up with a block of cement and the thick, wooden table, silent in the middle of the room. I could hear the worry of footsteps, skittering back and forth. More rats, only this time they were walled up inside my head.

I stood up and moved closer. Light played off the table's surface. I touched a gouge in the wood. Memories ran like a pulse through my fingertips. I stayed with it for as long as I could. Then I backed off and sat down again. After a while I switched off the basement light and locked the door behind me as I left.

Dinner was frozen pizza and a cold beer in the kitchen. After that I went upstairs, stripped off my muddy clothes, and stood under the shower. The water was hot and felt good on my skin. It was past one by the time I got to bed. I'd TiVo'd a cooking show off the Food Network and turned it on. I didn't really cook and didn't like the show, but the host looked like my mom so I watched. Around three in the morning I went downstairs and walked into my backyard. I lay down on the grass, listened to the night, and smelled the dirt. I counted stars until the sky began to lighten in the east. Then I went back inside and got ready for the day.

12

The elevator clanked to a stop and the old man pushed the folding gate open. I stepped out first. Jake Havens followed close behind. We were on the third floor of the Cook County evidence warehouse. A layer of dust tickled my nose, and I could sense the massive height and depth of the room. The old man flicked on a flashlight and skewered us with it.

"You say you're from Medill?"

I nodded. "We're researching a murder."

The old man held the light close to his chest so it lit up his jack-o'-lantern grin. "You ever been up here?"

I shook my head. He scratched out a laugh and shuffled off. Jake's voice ran beside me like a dark current through a cold river. "Just act dumb. He'll get bored and leave. Then we get what we came for."

Somewhere in the darkness came a thump, followed by a low hum. Strands of light filtered down from the rafters, casting lopsided shadows on the rough brick. We were standing at the edge of a room that was maybe a football field long. Three double rows of green shelving stretched themselves the length of the room and all the way to the ceiling. The shelves were crammed with boxes of all sizes, dimensions, and colors. Some were labeled and taped up tight; others were cracked and ripped, their sides oozing contents. Stuffed between the boxes were more plastic bags, as well as individual items. In a single glance, we saw a meat slicer, a toilet seat, and a set of hammers. I picked up a black pot. It didn't have an evidence tag on it or any other identifying feature.

"Why do you suppose this is here?" I said.

"It's a murder weapon," Havens said and held up a sheaf of papers he'd found on a nearby shelf. "On February eighth, 1978, Jessica Watson threw hot water over her husband and scalded him to death. Jessica claimed she was abused and had acted in self-defense."

"What happened?"

Havens flipped forward a couple of pages. "At trial, the prosecution showed there were second- and third-degree burns over most of the husband's upper body but none on his wrists." He looked up and smiled. "Want to guess why?"

"No idea."

"She tied him up with rope before dumping the water on him."

"And the rope protected his wrists?"

Havens handed me the case summary. "Jessica got forty to life. Pretty light, if you ask me."

I glanced through the report and back at the pot with newfound respect.

"Getting a good eyeful?" Our guide was back, the sour smell of sweat and cheap tobacco celebrating his arrival. He took the iron pot from me and put it back on the shelf. "Don't be touching anything unless you're wearing gloves. What year did you say?"

"Nineteen eighty-eight," Havens said.

"This way." He walked us halfway down the room. "First two digits of the case number tell you the year of the crime. Eighty-eight starts here. And make sure to use the gloves." He pointed to a box of latex gloves stuffed up on one of the shelves. "Copy machine is by the elevator. Bring all your copies downstairs when you're done, and I'll sign you out."

We listened as the elevator thumped its way back to the ground floor. Then we were alone. Just us and the murders.

"Why did you tell him 1988?" I said.

"Because I didn't want him to know what year we were actually after."

"A little paranoid?"

"Come on." Havens led me down one row and up the next, reeling through a decade of Chicago crime. Finally, we came to stacks of boxes with case numbers that began with "98" and "99." We each took a row. Havens, of course, found it.

"Here." He pulled out a white evidence box numbered 98-2425. The label read: WINGATE HOMICIDE. The box itself was sealed up tight. Havens took out the knife he'd flashed in the woods the night before.

"You came prepared," I said.

He cut the seal on the box without a word. Inside we found a handful of folders fat with documents.

"I thought Sarah was going after the paper trail?" I said.

"She's gonna get whatever documents were filed with the court," Havens said. "These must have been their working files."

I pulled out one of the folders. It contained various police reports filed at the time of the disappearance, along with a sketch of the neighborhood. Jake dug deeper in the box and came out with a clear plastic evidence bag tagged the date the body was found and bearing a scribble that was some cop's initials. Inside the bag, a young boy looked at us out of a thin wooden frame. The glass in the frame was cracked; the boy's smile splintered in a dozen different directions.

"There was a lot more stuff here at one time," I said.

"No kidding." Havens turned the box around so I could get a look at what was scrawled in marker on the side.

WINGATE EVIDENCE

I OF 4

"So we have some documents, a photo, and three missing boxes of evidence?" I said.

"Looks like it." Havens had found a small stepladder and started to climb.

"What are you doing?"

"Maybe the other boxes were misfiled," he said, poking around on one of the upper shelves.

"Or maybe the county destroyed them. How about the old man downstairs?"

"How about him?" Havens stared down at me from atop the ladder. He was already covered in dust.

"We could ask him to put a trace on the boxes," I said.

"Yeah, I'm sure they have everything up here on computers."

"Don't be an asshole."

Havens came down off the ladder and wiped a grimy line of sweat off his forehead. "Seriously, would you trust that guy? There's nothing up there that says WINGATE."

"So you think the shirt's gone?" I said.

"We don't have it, that's for damn sure." Havens picked up the box we'd found and started walking back down the aisle.

"Where are you going?" I said.

Havens answered without looking back. "To make some copies."

I unpacked the files and laid them out on a table. Police reports, witness statements, sketches of the crime scene, investigators' notes.

"Cops call this their murder book," Havens said and began to make copies. I picked up an autopsy report and leafed through it. According to the coroner, Skylar Wingate had been stabbed three times, none fatal, and strangled with a long green cord before he was put in the water. The cord was still around his neck when the police found him.

"Why dump a kid in the river and then pull him out and bury him?" I said.

"I told you," Havens said. "The killer's got some fixation with water."

"Why?"

"These guys sometimes have rituals. Things they like to do during each kill."

We talked about the body of a ten-year-old boy like so much chattel. In the worn corridors of the evidence warehouse, it seemed perfectly normal.

"You think there's any chance the body we found in the cave was done by the same guy who did Wingate?" I said.

Havens shook his head. "Not likely."

"Why not?"

"Like you said last night, Wingate was fourteen years ago."

"So you think we just stumbled onto the cave by coincidence?"

"Didn't say that. Remember, I'm the one who led you to the woods in the first place. By the way, did you notice there was nothing about the body in the papers today?"

"Might have been too late for the morning edition."

"Nothing online either," Havens said.

"You think the cops are keeping it quiet?"

"Either that or no one cares."

I leafed through the rest of the autopsy report. No obvious sexual trauma, although the coroner did note evidence of bruising, identified as possible bite marks, around the shoulders and neck. I put down the report and picked up a small square envelope. I could feel the stiff edges of the snapshots inside and pulled them out.

"Crime scene?" Havens said.

I shook my head and shuffled through the stack of photos.

"What is it?"

I looked up. The copier flashed and thumped, throwing angled shapes across Havens's face. "Take a look for yourself." I pushed one of the photos across. Skylar Wingate sat on a stripped-down cot. His hands lay in his lap, one folded over the other. His hair was wet and combed back from his forehead. His eyes searched the corners of the photograph, looking for a familiar face, someone who'd take him home.

"Looks like the guy took pictures," I said, "before he killed him."

I fed Havens another photo. We'd moved closer. The ten-year-old was belly down on the bed, hands and feet bound, head craned awkwardly toward the camera. The green cord was around his neck now and taut, one end trailing off the edge of the picture. The boy's face was quiet, eyes still large with fear but resigned to whatever might come. The next three photos were all tight shots. My eyes glided over each. Features bulging, as the rope tightened. Lips parting. The silent hiss of the boy's breath. I glanced at Havens. He seemed a mile across the table. I pushed the photos away.

"You all right?" Havens said.

I nodded.

"Nasty prick." Havens rearranged the shots in the probable sequence in which they were taken. "Must have rigged the noose up so Skylar hung in bits and pieces. That way he could snap off pictures as the kid strangled."

"Why would he do that?" I said.

"Same reason he buried Wingate's body instead of leaving it out on the riverbank. So he could revisit the crime scene. Revisit his trophy."

"Why leave them behind with the body?"

"To show off, maybe. Make a statement to the cops. He probably took other pictures he kept with him."

I moved the photos around so I could see them better under the light. Then I put them back in their envelope. Havens was working the copier.

"How long is this going to take?" I said, my voice suddenly rich with anxiety.

"The copies? Half hour. Maybe less. You in a hurry?"

"I'm fine." I wasn't fine. I wanted nothing more than to be out of the county's dusty tomb—away from hammers and ropes; autopsy reports weighing spleens, hearts, and livers; and the long, gray evidence boxes, stacked up around me like so many coffins.

"I've got to head back to my apartment after we get done," Havens said.

"Okay."

"You think you can take this stuff in your car?" He pointed to the pile of copies he was making.

"Why don't you take it?"

Havens stopped copying. "What's the matter with you?"

"Nothing. I'm just not crazy about being here."

"Really?" Havens looked around the warehouse like, *Where else would anyone want to be.*

"I can take the stuff," I said. "Let's just hurry up."

It actually took us the better part of an hour to finish. As we walked into the sunshine, I shook off the malaise of the warehouse and thought about what we'd found. I still wasn't sure about all the questions, but I had a funny feeling the answers might be buried somewhere in the documents we loaded into my car. Someone else, apparently, had the exact same feeling. Except they didn't think it was funny at all.

13

I'd just come up on the intersection of Roosevelt and Canal when I saw the blue flashers in my rearview mirror. A voice came over the PA system.

"Turn off onto Canal, sir."

I drove for a block and a half before pulling into an empty lot near the Pacific Garden Mission. An unmarked black sedan stuck to my bumper the whole way. A couple of bums were hanging around outside Pacific. Otherwise, we were alone. A middle-aged white guy in a shiny suit got out of the car. His partner, a little younger and black, stayed inside. The one who got out was all forearms and fists. He had thinning red hair, gray sideburns, and dark sunglasses. He gave me a quick look at a silver detective's star and put it back in his pocket.

"License and registration."

I handed over my license and dug my registration out of the glovie. He took both without a word and headed back to his car. I pulled out my phone and punched in a number. Sarah's voice mail picked up on the first ring. I watched the cop car in the rearview mirror as I spoke.

"Sarah, it's Ian. Listen, I'm driving back from the evidence warehouse and just got pulled over on Canal Street, south of Roosevelt. It's an unmarked car. I can't read the tag number, and I have no idea why they stopped me." The sedan door swung open, and the detective got out. "He's coming back. I'll call you when I can."

I cut the line and shoved the phone into my shirt pocket.

"Step out of the car, Mr. Joyce."

I got out.

"Give me the phone."

"Why?"

He pulled it out of my pocket and checked the last number I'd dialed. Then he slipped the cell into his pocket and put a hand on the butt of his gun.

"Do you know why I pulled you over?"

"No sir, I don't." My heart was fluttering inside my rib cage. My voice sounded strong.

"You made a lane switch back on Roosevelt and failed to use your turn signal."

"Turn signal, huh?"

"That's right."

I couldn't help but look at the paperwork from the warehouse, sitting in the backseat of my car.

"I'm going to need to ask you a few questions," the detective said.

"How about you just write me a ticket?"

"Are you carrying any contraband in the vehicle?"

"Contraband?"

"Drugs, firearms, things of that nature?"

I shook my head.

"Do you mind if we take a look?"

"Actually, I do."

"That right?"

"Yes. And I'd like my cell phone back if that's okay."

The detective smiled behind his sunglasses and dropped his voice as if someone in the empty lot might be listening. "Here's how this works. You consent to the search of your car, or my partner calls in a canine unit. We cuff you and put you in a squad car until the dogs show up. Probably about an hour or two. Then we run the fucking dog around for five minutes and, surprise, surprise, he hits for the possible presence of contraband. Then we search your car anyway. Only it's two hours from now, and we make it hurt. So, it's your choice, smart guy."

Ten minutes later, I was sitting in the backseat of the sedan as the two Chicago detectives opened up the doors to my car, popped the hood, and began to take things apart.

At the end of the day, they confiscated twenty-three dollars I had in my pocket and another eight in singles they found in the center console as "possible drug money." They also took an empty gas can, a Cubs cooler with three warm beers in it, and all of the paperwork from the backseat. The white detective leaned on the hood of my car and wrote out a receipt for the confiscated property.

"Can I get your names?" I said.

"It will be on the receipt."

"Can I ask why you took all the files from my backseat? I'm a student at Northwestern, and they're part of a class project. I don't see how they could be considered contraband."

"It's all explained here." The detective ripped off the receipt and held it between his fingers. "You have thirty days to file a petition for the return of your items. If you don't file a petition, the confiscated materials become the property of the government. If you do file, we'll either return the items or you can pursue a civil suit to contest the forfeiture. Is that clear?"

"No. Nothing's clear."

"I'd suggest you head straight home, Mr. Joyce. And be more careful using your turn signal in the future."

The two detectives walked back to their car and drove off. I studied the receipt they'd given me. There was no explanation as to why they'd seized anything. Just a lot of checked boxes indicating they had. I stuffed the receipt into my pocket and climbed into my car. Five minutes later, I was on the highway. The white detective had given me back my phone. Sarah had left three messages. She sounded concerned. If nothing else, that made me feel better.

14

I'd just pulled up to my house when Sarah called again.

"Where are you?" she said.

"Just got home. Why?"

"Jake and I drove down to Canal and Roosevelt looking for you."

My heart leaped a touch at the idea of Sarah Gold getting into her car and searching for me. The fact that Havens was her passenger? Not so thrilling, but I'd take what I could get.

"Where are you now?" I said.

"We stopped at the police station down here. They have no record of your being pulled over."

"Maybe it's not in the system yet."

"The cop says it should be. What was the badge number of the officer?"

"It was a plainclothes detective." I pulled out the crumpled receipt and gave it a second look. "I can't read his name or his number."

"Hold on a second, Jake wants to talk to you."

"Wait . . ." Too late. Havens came on the line.

"Are you guys at the police station?" I said.

"We just left."

"You gave them my name?"

"Yes."

"Did they ask for yours?"

There was a pause as Havens asked Sarah a question I couldn't make out, then he came back on the line. "Neither of us gave a name. Why?"

"I don't know."

"So you have no way of identifying these guys?" Havens said.

"I didn't get a look at their license plate, if that's what you're asking."

Silence.

"I'm guessing they pulled me over so they could grab the records."

"Seems hard to believe," Havens said.

"Come up with a better reason."

"That case has been sitting there for more than a decade. Anyone could have gone down and looked at it."

"Yeah, but maybe no one did. If I'm right, the old man at the warehouse made a call. Or maybe they were already waiting for us outside." The more I reduced my theory to words, the better it sounded. "Are you and Sarah headed back?"

"Yeah."

"Let's get together tomorrow," I said.

"For what? We've got nothing to talk about."

I checked my eyes in the rearview mirror. "Don't be so sure about that."

"What does that mean?"

"We'll talk tomorrow."

I clicked off, got out of the car, and walked up the path to my house. The lawyer had told me to sell the place. Bank the money. Buy a condo downtown. Or both. What do lawyers know? I went into the kitchen and sat at the table. I could hear her key in the door. A yell that she was home. My mom wasn't much of a cook, so we'd go out and get McDonald's. When I got older, high school age, she told me I should go out with friends. But I didn't care. I liked to eat with my mom. Then college came. Right on schedule, she got sick. I got up from the chair and opened a cabinet. There was a can of soup there and some crackers. I poured the soup into a pot and lit the stove with a match. It was an old stove. Lawyer probably wanted to get rid of that, too.

I walked into the living room. The wooden floor creaked under my feet. I sat on the couch and reread the letter she'd left with the lawyer. Then I put it down and picked up a framed picture I kept on an end table. It was an old print ad for Tide that ran in the *Trib*. My mom was the star, a young girl pulling sheets off a clothesline. Her eyes were wrinkled, and the sun was on her face.

"What are you staring at, Ian?"

I fumbled the picture and heard the crack of glass as it hit the floor. My mom stood in front of me.

"Don't worry about it," she said and began to pick up the pieces of glass, jagged and smeared with blood. Then she got a bandage from the bathroom and wrapped my hand where I'd cut it. When she was finished, she looked up at me. Her mouth was stitched into a frightened smile, and I could see my reflection in the black of her eyes.

"How are you?" she said.

"I'm fine, Ma."

"You look thin."

"I started school this week. Graduate school at Medill."

"Is it fall yet?"

"Summer quarter, Ma."

"That's nice." She sat down beside me. Memories flocked and swarmed around us. She crooked a finger and drew me closer. I moved as if on a string.

"I should have protected you, Ian. Both of you."

The wind rattled a window somewhere in protest.

"You did what you could."

"I should have done better."

Her voice was unraveling. I leaned in, trying to catch the words as they crumbled in my hands. And then I was outside her bedroom, in the hallway upstairs, my palm flat against the door. She stood on the other side, fingers tracing mine against the worn wood, listening to the rise and fall of my chest, counting each breath as her own.

"Ma?" My voice was that of a boy, still drawing warm terror from his mother's breast. The door creaked open and she stood there, in a black wind, one hand resting on a small, white coffin.

I woke with a start. The light outside was almost gone, houses across the street edged in thin lines of pink. The smell of smoke crept through the house. I got up and ran into the kitchen. The soup had cooked off, and the pot was burned on the bottom. I cleaned up as best I could and opened a window. Then I sat at the kitchen table and rubbed my temples with my fingers. Every now and then it happened. She'd be there, picking up the thread of a conversation we'd never had. Dreams like jagged pieces of shrapnel, cutting the wounds fresh. The doorbell rang, and I jumped. I couldn't remember the last time I'd heard it ring. I put my mom's letter away and hustled to the door. Sarah Gold stood on the porch. First, a visit from my dead mother. Now, Sarah.

"Just thought I'd come by," she said. "See how you were doing."

"Thanks. I just woke up."

"Oh. Maybe I should come back?"

"No, no. Come on in."

And so Sarah Gold walked into my house. She seemed larger than life at school. In my living room, her smile threatened to melt the wallpaper off the walls. She sat on the couch and looked around. I sat across from her.

"Sorry," I said, waving away the smell of scorched metal and plastic. "I was cooking something and it burned."

"You live alone?" she said.

"Pretty much, yeah. How about you?"

"I live in the city. North Side. You seem a little out of it."

I gave myself an invisible shake. "I'm fine. Just half asleep."

Sarah gave the place another look. I felt an urgent need to fill the yawning chasm of quiet.

"I grew up here," I said. "I know, it's weird. A guy living in the house he grew up in."

"I didn't say that." Her voice had softened; her smile invited me in.

"My mom lived here," I said. "She lived here with me."

"Oh . . ."

"She passed last year."

Sarah reached out and touched my sleeve. "I'm so sorry, Ian."

I felt a dry patch in my throat and sudden tears stinging the backs of my eyes. Outside of the undertakers, not many people had ever told me they were sorry. But Sarah Gold had. And it caught me good.

"Thanks," I said.

"Is your dad around?"

"He passed a long time ago."

"I don't mean to pry . . ."

I brushed her concerns aside. "She suffered from early-onset dementia. Be there one minute and gone the next. Everyone at the funeral told me it was a blessing."

We were quiet again.

"Was this all going on . . . during undergrad?"

"Yeah. But it's cool."

It wasn't cool. Nothing about coming home every night to a nurse we couldn't afford and my mom, semiconscious and hooked up to a bunch of tubes, was cool. Not at any age. And definitely not when you were eighteen and a freshman in college. I let myself touch the anger for a moment. Allowed it to mingle with the grief. Then the guilt set in, and I put it all away.

"I'm so sorry, Ian."

"Like I said, don't worry about it. But now you know why I live here." I got up from the couch. "You want something to drink?"

"No, thanks." A car passed by the front of the house. Sarah seemed to watch it through the living room walls. "Yeah, okay. Maybe a glass of water?"

I got her some water with ice. Myself, a Coke.

"You want to talk about today?" she said.

"You first. Tell me about the records center."

"Pretty boring, actually."

"Really?" I took a sip and felt the spring inside unwind a little. Boring was exactly what I needed.

"They had a file on Harrison," Sarah said. "Briefs, pleadings, trial transcripts. Some documents that were entered into evidence."

"And?"

"It had been redacted to hell. Almost all of the substantive information was blacked out."

"Is that unusual?"

"I asked the clerk, but she had no idea." Sarah zipped open her backpack and pulled out a stack of papers. "I made copies of some things, but I wouldn't get my hopes up."

"You show Havens what you got?"

She nodded.

"What did he say?"

"He said he was working on an angle."

"Huh." I thumbed through her stuff. Sarah was right. It seemed pretty much useless.

"I think we might be wasting our time," she said.

I looked up. "On Harrison?"

"Yes."

"I disagree."

"Why?"

"First of all, if you believe the cops stopped me to get that paperwork, then someone's scared."

"But it's not evidence."

"Second, there might be a way to get back some of the stuff I lost today."

"How?"

"Hang on." I went into the kitchen and came back with a pen and pad of paper.

"You going to write something?" she said.

"Not yet. For right now we need to sit and be quiet."

A light flush stained her cheeks and a small smile played across Sarah's lips. "Quiet, you say?"

"Absolute quiet."

"What are we going to do?"

"*We* aren't going to do anything. I'm going to relax. You just sit."

I settled myself in an old leather recliner and closed my eyes. My body softened. My heart slowed. I counted forty-two beats a minute. Then thirty-seven. Somewhere Sarah fidgeted, but I was already slipping under. Thirty-five beats. I focused on my breathing. Inhale through one nostril. Exhale out the other. Flesh and bones melted away until only the core remained. The thump of my heart. The pump in my lungs. The third floor of the Cook County warehouse flickered across the back of my eyelids and came to life. I watched patiently, as if through a sheer curtain. Files from the Wingate case sat on a crooked wooden table. Havens stood to one side, making his copies. I pushed the curtain aside. The colors flared and hurt my eyes until I had to retreat. I waited a moment and tried again. This time the images came into a slow focus. The Wingate files were laid out on the table. Lines of dark print. Drawings. Scrawled notes and numbers. I saw each page distinctly. And yet all at once. My scalp tingled. My fingers itched. The images flashed past until they became a blur. Then there was nothing but heaviness. The download had finished.

I blinked my eyes open. Sarah was staring at me.

"How long has it been?" I said.

She checked her phone. "Ten minutes?"

I picked up a pen and began to write. She started to say something, but I stopped her. A half hour later, I'd finished. Sarah leafed through a dozen pages of scribble. Not perfect, but I figured I'd gotten back 60 percent of what the cops had taken.

"You have a photographic memory?" She was looking at me like I might be radioactive.

"If only. I have what they call a highly selective, short-term memory that has some eidetic components to it. If I focus and visualize, I can sometimes recall things for a very short period of time. Then they're gone forever. I can also do numbers. See different combinations of digits, equations in my head."

"You're *Good Will Hunting*."

"Hardly."

Sarah scooted a little closer. "Names, phone numbers. You've even reconstructed some of the autopsy sketches."

I went to the bathroom for some aspirin. Whatever kind of memory I had, it always gave me a headache. This one seemed especially bad. When I returned, Sarah was typing away on her iPhone.

"What are you doing?"

She hit SEND and looked up. "Just told Jake Havens we've gotten back our notes from the evidence warehouse. And we have a genius in the class."

"I only got sixty percent of what we lost."

"Close enough. Besides, the genius stuff will kill him. You want to go through all this? Maybe try to clean it up?"

"Might as well."

For the next three hours Sarah and I translated what I'd written into a coherent narrative. When we were finished, we sat back and read. The first few pages were mostly descriptions of the crime scene, comments by investigators on pieces of evidence and possible leads. I'd been able to recall some details from Harrison's arrest report and the bare bones of a memo I'd glimpsed from the files of the Cook County state's attorney. The latter summarized the blow-by-blow of James Harrison's trial. Best I could tell, there hadn't been much of one.

The county's case against Harrison consisted of an eyewitness named Bobby Atkinson who saw a man and a boy near Peterson Avenue at four-thirty in the afternoon on the day Skylar disappeared. The man fit Harrison's description and was wearing a black T-shirt and jeans. According to Atkinson, the boy looked a lot like Skylar. The state also presented evidence of a bloodstain on Harrison's jeans that was matched for type to the boy. DNA testing was available in Cook County in 1998, but neither the state nor the defense requested it. Harrison declined to take the stand in his own defense and offered no clear alibi. The entire proceeding took a day and a half. The jury deliberated for less than an hour. I dropped my notes onto the coffee table.

"Guilty or not, this guy didn't get the trial he deserved," I said and rubbed my eyes. "What time is it?"

"A little past eleven. You must be tired."

"I'm not that bad."

"How about we get out of here? Go get a drink?"

"Nevin's?"

"I've got something better in mind." Sarah was smiling when she said it.

15

The vodka was cold, and the bottle passed easily between us.

"I love it out here at night." Sarah dug her feet down into the sand. We were sitting on an empty beach, less than a mile from Fisk Hall. The wind was up, and the lake was crested in white. The surf moaned in the darkness.

"You come here a lot?" I said.

"Sometimes. When it's like this." She held out her hand, and I passed the Absolut. I'd found it, cold and lonely, in my freezer. Sarah took a sip and handed it back.

"You ever been in love, Ian?"

My response was a grin that was lopsided and leaking at the edges.

"What was her name?" Sarah said.

"Never mind."

"Why do you hold back?"

"What does that mean?"

"You hold back. Pieces of yourself. In class. Out of class. Now, when we're just talking."

I waggled the bottle in front of her. "I think you've had enough."

"I'm serious."

"So am I."

"Four years in school and no one ever knew you. Hardly anything."

"And you think that's my fault?"

"I didn't say that." She edged a toe through the sand and kept her eyes down as she spoke. "Is it because of your mom?" She looked up. "I'm sorry. Should I not talk about that?"

"If you shouldn't talk about it, then don't. If you do talk about it, don't ask for permission after the fact."

"Ian . . ."

"You think I just started existing because you're suddenly aware of me?"

"That's not what I meant."

I knew it wasn't what she meant. And I hated that it had turned ugly. "Don't worry about it." I wiped my mouth. She looked over carefully.

"I'm serious, Sarah. My mom's situation was what it was. Did I keep to myself because of it?" I shrugged. "Maybe, but I'm not complaining."

"It's okay to complain."

"I know that." I took another hit from the bottle, desperate to regain that Absolut glow. "Let's talk about something else."

"Like what?"

"I don't care."

"Ian . . ."

"It all right, Sarah. Really."

We sat some more and let the night settle around us. We were close by the water, and the breeze kept us dry.

"Can I tell you something else?" she said.

"Sure."

"I'm glad we met. Even if it did take four years plus." Her smile lit up the darkness between us, and suddenly everything was all right again.

"Me, too."

"Good." She leaned across and kissed me lightly. Easily. It tasted like citrus and sand. Then she was on her feet.

"Where are you going?" I said.

"For a swim."

"Bullshit."

She turned and padded silently toward the water, shedding clothes as she went. I got up and followed. I'd have been a fool not to.

16

The man with yellow eyes sat on the beach, a hundred paces south. Might as well have been a mile away for all they knew. He could tell they were drinking and imagined how the rest of it might go. But that didn't interest him. Unless he decided to kill them. Then everything changed.

The girl got up and began to run in his direction, at an angle toward the water. He watched her strip off her shirt. Then her shorts. The boy sat in the sand, like a fucking idiot. Finally he got up and hobbled, almost bent at the waist, toward the surf. The man with the yellow eyes understood now what he'd sensed in the woods. All in all, it made perfect sense. The man crept forward, drifting like a dark sigh along the water's edge and taking a small inhale before slipping beneath a wave. He stroked to within fifty feet of the two of them and surfaced. Then he treaded water. And listened.

17

I could just see her as she hit the surf, body arched, cutting into the face of a wave as it broke and popping up on the other side. And then she was swimming, a strong freestyle stroke, up and over the next roller. Best I could tell from the trail of clothes, Sarah Gold still had her bra and panties on. Part of me was disappointed. Part was relieved. I stripped down to my underwear and tested the temperature.

It was barely July in Chicago. The lake hadn't warmed up a whole lot when the sun was out. At night it was out of the question. Except, apparently, for Sarah. I put a foot in and gasped. She was maybe twenty yards out now and turning to look back. Cold be damned, I ran until I was waist-deep. I couldn't feel my legs, but that was okay. She rose up out of the water and waved. I took a deep breath and plunged into a wave. Sarah was waiting on the other side.

"Sobers you up, huh?" She whipped her head free of water and tucked her hair behind her ears.

"Freezing."

She ducked into a wave and paddle kicked back out. "Stay in the water. You'll keep warm."

I wasn't much of a swimmer, but I followed anyway. I was fairly certain I'd follow Sarah Gold all the way to Canada if she had a mind. Or die trying, with a big smile on my face. We paddled past the line of surf. The water wasn't as rough out here, and we bobbed up and down, treading water as the rollers swept past.

"I used to lifeguard every summer," Sarah said, her voice lonely in the lake at night.

"Where?"

She nodded in the general direction of Michigan. "Harbor Springs."

I knew about Harbor Springs. Or at least had seen the pictures. Clear blue water, deep, sandy beaches, and carpets of thick grass rolled up to gabled homes with long sweeping porches and wicker furniture. Men with white teeth and heavy gold watches. Women with flawless complexions and wide-brimmed hats. Everyone tanned, living forever, and drinking gin and tonics.

"Heard it's nice," I said.

"It's where I'm from."

"What does that mean?"

"Nothing. It's just that everyone's from somewhere, and you wear it like a second skin. Anyway, it's a long way from Chicago."

"Yes, it is."

We treaded water for a while longer. The sky was black and deep, impossibly huge, with a handful of pale stars tossed across it. A breeze kicked up around us, and I felt my body spasm in the cold. Sarah seemed immune to it.

"I'm not the greatest swimmer," I said.

"You're doing fine."

A wave caught me on the chin, and I spit out a little water. "Yeah, well, it's fucking cold."

She laughed. "Come here. I'll warm you up."

Sarah moved close and wrapped her legs around mine. I could feel the strength in her thighs as she gripped me.

"In lifeguard training they taught us how to share body heat." She spit a small bit of water from her mouth.

"Oh, yeah?" I could hear the strain and catch in my voice.

"Yeah." Sarah moved closer, rubbing her entire body against mine. The water temperature might have been sixty degrees, but things were happening. And Sarah couldn't help but feel it. "It's critical that we stay warm," she said. Her face was inches from mine, both arms draped around my shoulders.

"You think so?"

We bobbed up and down on a wave as she nodded. I felt myself falling toward her. This kiss was the real thing, long, deep, and wet. I could feel her breasts against my chest, her nipples hard through the fabric. We pulled apart but kept our bodies touching. Her eyes were closed, face upturned and edged in moonlight. "That was nice." Sarah opened her eyes and splashed me. "Race you back." Then she was gone again, ducking under the water and knifing away.

I followed her back in, the waves pushing us home. She streamed up and out of the water. I struggled in the surf, which, truth be told, wasn't the worst thing in the world. I needed a little time for Mother Nature to settle before stepping onto the beach. So I wallowed and watched. Sarah walked without a trace of self-consciousness. Body, tanned and cut. Legs, lean muscle, perfectly proportioned. She was beautiful. As beautiful as she'd ever be. And I suddenly felt sad because of it.

Sarah picked up her clothes, found a rock to sit on, and got dressed. When it was safe, I came out of the water. She was waiting up the beach.

"That was fun." She handed me the vodka, but I wasn't as interested. "Fun" wasn't the word I was looking for, although I certainly would have accepted it an hour ago. Had the stakes shifted? Sarah Gold and Ian Joyce? A couple? I chuckled and changed my mind about the bottle.

"What are you laughing at?" she said.

"'A man's reach should never exceed his grasp.'"

"Robert Browning. And that's not what he said. Or meant. In fact, quite the opposite."

"Excuse me?"

"The quote is: 'A man's reach should exceed his grasp, or what's a heaven for?' I was an English lit major, with a concentration in English poetry."

"I stand corrected."

She gave me a playful push. We started walking, hands linked loosely. Not meaning much, except everything. After about a hundred yards, we sat down again. I thought I saw a shadow along the water's edge, but it was just a breeze off the lake. Sarah found a smooth stone and tossed it into the darkness.

"It won't be like this for much longer, you know."

"Be like what?"

She flicked a hand at a scatter of lights in the distance. "Like this. Northwestern. College. Grad school. Make-believe."

"That's what you think this is?"

"Absolutely. And a lot of people freak at the prospect of it ending."

"You don't seem like the type that's gonna freak."

"No?" She rolled over on the flat of her stomach and played sand through her fingers. "First semester, freshman year. I'm sitting on a bench outside Norris. All by myself. Middle of the day. People walk by. I smile. They don't know I'm alive. I tell myself everything's going to be fine. I've always been popular. Then I look down at my hands. They're clutching my purse in a death grip. Heart's beating a tattoo through my chest."

"Why?"

"My world was getting bigger. Would I measure up?"

"You measure up just fine, Sarah."

"Four years later, sure. But there's always the next step. The next level."

"You afraid of that?"

"Sometimes. Other times, I'm desperate for it. For anything real."

A wild shiver of wind ran through us.

"It's getting chilly," I said.

"What happened today, with the two detectives, you think that's something . . ."

"Real? Hard to say. Sure felt like it."

"Havens scares me a little," she said.

"He probably should."

"Let's talk about something else."

"Okay."

She rubbed the edge of her foot against mine. "I'm glad we took a swim."

"Me, too." I paused. "Maybe it should be our secret."

"Are you ashamed of me, Ian Joyce?"

"Please."

She kissed me on the cheek and traced the curve of my face. "It would never work, anyway." Her voice hovered now, barely above a tipsy whisper.

"I know."

"But it could have been fun."

"Maybe it's better not to talk about it."

She was quiet again, and we listened to the surf.

"Friends?" she said.

"For sure."

We sat in the dark and watched the waves, a mostly empty bottle and our stillborn romance lying on the sand between us. After a while, it got too cold, even for Sarah. I offered her my jacket, and she took it. We held hands and walked the rest of the way back to campus. I made sure she found her car. Then I walked home. My head hurt from the alcohol, and I wondered how well I'd sleep. But it wasn't a problem. I closed my eyes and the waves were there, heavy and thick, sweeping me into the deep reaches of the lake, where I waited for the rip to take me under.

18

I woke to the sound of a knock downstairs. Jake Havens was at my front door.

"It's Sunday morning, Havens. What do you want?"

"Thought we'd pick up Sarah and grab some breakfast. Unless, of course, she's already here?" He shot a playful look up the stairs.

"Fuck you." I pushed him into the kitchen. "Wait here while I get dressed."

I pulled on some clothes, listening for footsteps as Havens explored my house. But I found him right where I'd left him, at the kitchen table, reading the morning *Trib*.

"Still nothing about the body in the cave," he said and pushed the paper across. "By the way, why do you have me copying things when you have a photographic memory?"

"I don't have a photographic memory."

"Show me what you came up with."

"What about Sarah?"

"She can wait."

I pulled out my notes. Havens pored through them while I made coffee. When he'd finished, he stacked the pages into a neat pile and folded his hands over them.

"Good stuff, Joyce. Stuff I can use."

"I'm thrilled."

Sarcasm appeared to be yet another thing that had no effect on my classmate.

"You want to see what I'm working on?" he said.

"Lead on."

We walked out to his car. Havens popped the trunk. Inside were three Bankers Boxes. I lifted one out. Heavy. Scrawled in Magic Marker on the side were names, dates, and case numbers.

"I've been busy," Havens said with a grin.

"No kidding. What do we got here?"

"Let's bring them inside."

We lugged the boxes into my living room.

"Did Sarah tell you about the records center?" I said.

"She said everything in the files was cut up and blacked out. Tell me about the cops that stopped you."

I gave him the firsthand account. Havens listened closely.

"Someone's worried," he said.

"My thoughts exactly."

He opened one of the boxes and began to remove files.

"What is all this?" I said.

"Ever heard of ViCAP?"

"No."

"Violent Criminal Apprehension Program. It's an FBI program that analyzes crimes and sorts them into different categories."

"What kind of categories?"

"All kinds. Guys that like to tie up their victims. Ones that like to use a knife. Strangle. Different variations of sexual assault. ViCAP identifies the signature of a crime and then matches it up with similar cases. Gives the police a way to look for patterns."

"And you have access to ViCAP?"

"One of my law profs at Chicago does. I told him I wanted to get a jump on the assholes from Evanston." Havens winked. "He let me run Harrison's case through the system. Pretty interesting."

Havens pulled out a laptop and powered it up. "I punched in all the signature details I could think of. Age of the victim. Kidnapping.

School. Proximity to water. Strangulation, drowning. Some evidence of a knife."

"Yeah?"

"Then I ran a search in the Chicagoland area. Anything within a five-year window of Skylar Wingate."

My head felt heavy, and my skin itched. I wanted Havens to get to the punch line. The barrister in him, however, was nothing if not methodical.

"I picked five years because I thought it was a reasonable amount of time to expect a killer to be active. If you look at the research on most serial killers—"

"What did you find, Jake?"

Havens pointed to two case numbers highlighted in a document he'd opened up on his laptop. "Two cases. Within three years of Wingate's death."

"How close are they?"

"You tell me." Havens reached into one of the boxes and pulled out a folder with a green tab. On the cover was a picture of a kid, smiling in his Little League uniform. "Nineteen ninety-six. Billy Scranton from Indiana. Ran away when he was thirteen. Six months later, they found him partially buried in the forest preserve. Maybe a mile from Skylar. He'd been drowned. Possibly strangled."

A second jacket hit the table. On the cover was a blurry shot of a black kid.

"Ninety-seven. Richmond Allen. Fourteen. Another runaway, from Texas. They found him in a wooded area on the South Side. Twenty miles from Caldwell Woods, but near a lake. He had a rope around his neck. Just like Skylar. And water in his lungs."

"No one ever connected the cases?"

Havens shook his head.

"And they're still unsolved?"

"That's where it gets interesting." Havens opened up a second box and pulled out a stack of red-tabbed folders. Where did he get all this shit? And where did he get the time?

"Both cases were 'solved.'" Havens made quote marks in the air with his fingers. "Remember, this was still the early days of DNA. Very difficult. Very expensive. Barely understood."

"So no DNA requests in either case?"

"That's right. In the Scranton case, they nailed the guy with fibers that allegedly came from his car and his coat. Wayne Williams sort of thing. Guy from Atlanta."

"I know who Wayne Williams is."

"In the Allen case, it was blood typing."

"What about witnesses?"

"No witnesses other than experts and cops. Public defenders in both trials."

"And where are the guys that got convicted?"

"One got life. The other got the needle. I'd give you their names, but it doesn't matter."

"Like hell it doesn't matter. We can talk to them. If we can establish their innocence and link them up with Wingate . . ."

"They were both killed in prison. After less than a year inside. My prof knew a guy from the Department of Corrections who was able to get me some details."

Havens turned the laptop around so I could read his notes. An inmate named Michael Laramore was found in his cell, strangled with a length of packing wire. A second inmate, Jason Tyson, was discovered in the prison shop area at Stateville. He had five masonry nails through his forehead. With James Harrison, that made three convictions and three bodies.

"What the fuck?" I said.

"No shit. You got any coffee left?"

Havens and I walked into my kitchen. He insisted on making a fresh pot, so I showed him where everything was. Then I went back into the living room and picked through his work. It wasn't hard to understand why Havens was number one at the University of Chicago Law School. While Sarah and I had cobbled together a dozen pages of half-remembered thoughts, our classmate had developed a plausible theory linking Wingate to two more murders, generated impressive backup, and summarized the salient points in a series of short memos. He came back into the living room with a hot cup of joe. I was leafing through the autopsy report on Billy Scranton. Underneath it was an initial police report. The Allen file contained a similar stash of documents.

"How'd you get all this case information?" I said.

"ViCAP allows you to access material from the actual murder file without making a direct request. Check this out." Havens pulled out copies of two photos and put them side by side.

"What are these?" I said.

"Bite marks. Both of these kids were bitten during the attack."

I stared at the pale bruised flesh. "Wingate's autopsy said he might have been bitten."

"I know." Havens tossed the photos on top of the other documents.

"Should they have caught this pattern?" I said. "Back in the day, I mean."

"Be kind of tough. These crimes were spread out over three years. And remember, the locals didn't have access to ViCAP back then to sort it all out."

"I guess," I said.

Havens took a sip and made a face. "How old are these beans?"

"Forget about the beans. What should we do with all of this?"

"We can put in a request with the county for the physical evidence on these two. But I'm betting they sanitized them, just like Wingate."

"Who's 'they'?"

"Whoever's behind the cover-up." Havens sat down at the table. "I've been thinking about this."

I gestured to the stacks of information surrounding us. "I can tell."

"We agree these three might have been the work of a single killer?"

"Agreed."

"And whoever he is, he's no longer active. Probably dead."

"Fourteen years ago, I don't know that he's dead, but probably not active."

"My point is this. Someone downtown framed these three guys and got away with it."

"Do you even know anyone downtown, Havens? I mean one person? One name?"

"Fuck you. I say we see where this takes us."

I looked down at the case files. The face of Billy Scranton looked back at me. Murdered at age thirteen.

"So we're going to take a pass on finding out who actually killed these kids?"

"If something pops about the killer, we'll go for it, of course. But for right now let's focus on what we do know. Someone in Cook County was in the business of framing innocent men and putting them up on death row."

"You tell Sarah about your theories?" I said.

"I gave her the basics."

"What about Z?"

"What about her?"

"Will she buy any of it?"

"She might not have a choice."

"What does that mean?"

Havens was about to respond when his laptop pinged with an e-mail. A few seconds later, my cell phone buzzed with a text. They were both from Z. It was Sunday morning, and she wanted us back in her classroom. Within the hour.

19

Sarah was waiting outside Fisk. She hugged both of us, giving me what felt like an extra squeeze and a wink. When it came to emotions, I was good at hiding them. Sarah Gold wasn't going to be a problem. At least that's what I told myself.

"You been here long?" Havens said.

"Five minutes." Sarah took a sip of her coffee. "What does Z want?"

I shook my head. "It's gotta be about the woods."

"Damn."

"Relax," Havens said. "I've got a plan."

We talked for ten minutes, then headed into class. Z raised her head as we filed in.

"Close the door, Mr. Joyce."

I did. Z took off her glasses and stared me down as I found a seat.

"I called you in this morning because there's something urgent we need to discuss." Z kept her eyes fixed on yours truly as she spoke.

Havens cleared his throat. "What is it?"

Z pulled out a plastic bag and held it pinched between her fingers. Inside was a wrinkled business card. "Recognize this?"

"We can't see it," Havens said.

She laid the Baggie flat on her desk. I got up from my seat and walked to the front of the room. Sarah and Havens crowded close beside me. The business card was bent at the edges and smudged with dirt, but I could make out the print just fine. The Medill crest. My name. My cell phone number.

"Mr. Joyce?" Z played a hand along the sealed edge of the bag as she talked. There was an orange sticker on the bag. Her fingers prevented me from reading it.

"That's my card," I said.

"Any idea where it was found?"

"Looks like I might have dropped it somewhere."

"Please sit down. All of you."

She waited until we'd taken our seats. Then she walked to the back of the room and opened the door. A cop came in. He didn't identify himself as a cop. He didn't need to. He had the look. Long and lean. Dark. Cool without trying. The kind of look actors in cop movies strive for. And never quite achieve. Except, of course, for De Niro.

The cop took a seat, positioning himself where he could keep an eye on all of us. Z walked back behind her desk and remained standing as she spoke.

"This is Chicago detective Vince Rodriguez. He works with Homicide." She let the last word rattle around the room for a couple of seconds before continuing. "He brought Mr. Joyce's business card to my attention. Ian, we need to talk about this, but I thought I'd give you, Sarah, and you, Jake, the opportunity to sit in or leave. As you see fit."

Sarah shifted in her seat. Havens clasped his hands behind his head and stared a bullet at Z. Rodriguez took it all in without ever moving his eyes.

"I think we're good where we are," Havens finally said. "As long as it's all right with Ian. And the detective."

Rodriguez floated to his feet. I could see the gun on his hip. A detective's star was clipped beside it.

"Ms. Zombrowski wanted you all here because she thinks you might be involved as a group. And this approach might save some time. I'm not sure, but we'll see. Ian . . ." Rodriguez turned to me. His face was largely impassive, except his eyes, which were darkly lit and relentlessly patient. It wasn't an easy face to talk to . . . especially when you were about to lie.

"Yes, sir?"

"The card. Do you remember losing it?"

"No, sir. I have a stack they gave us at the beginning of the quarter, so it would be tough."

Rodriguez chewed on that brilliant morsel for a bit. "No idea where we might have found it?"

I shrugged and turned my palms up. Rodriguez looked to my two classmates. They didn't offer much help. The detective sighed.

"Your card was found in Caldwell Woods." His eyes caught mine at the mention of the woods. "You know where that is?"

Havens cleared his throat. "We know where the woods are, Detective."

"Mister?"

"Havens. Jake Havens."

"You know where the woods are?"

"We've all been there, sir. In the last few days."

Z coughed. Rodriguez skewed his features into something resembling a question mark. Havens continued.

"A boy named Skylar Wingate was killed there years ago. I don't know if Z, Ms. Zombrowski, told you . . ." Havens paused a moment, allowing Z and her betrayal of her class to twist in the wind. "We're working on the case for this class. All three of us were in that part of the forest preserve. Two nights ago, around dusk. We found what we thought to be the boy's grave site, looked around for a bit, and left. Probably got there just before seven and stayed about an hour and a half."

Rodriguez was seated again. He'd taken out a notebook and was writing in it. For the first time, I noticed a small recorder, red light on, sitting on the table beside him. We waited until he finished. The detective looked up at Havens.

"That it?"

"We saw flashlights in the woods. Probably around eight, maybe later. We didn't know who it was and bugged out."

Rodriguez turned to me, then Sarah. "You two? Anything else?"

"Are you reopening the Wingate case?" I said.

"You don't get to ask the questions, Mr. Joyce. Where were you when you dropped the card?"

"I don't know."

"Take a guess."

"We found a small depression in the ground. Close to the water. We thought that was where Skylar had been buried. I remember kneeling down and searching the area." I shook my head. "Not sure what I was looking for, but I might have dropped the card there."

"We were also crashing through a lot of underbrush to get to the site," Sarah said. "He could have dropped it anywhere."

"How about a cave?" Rodriguez said.

Havens snuck me a look he shouldn't have. The detective didn't miss it.

"We never went near any cave," I said.

"You sure?"

"Yes, sir."

Rodriguez wrote the lie down in his notebook and closed it. "I think that's all for now."

"For now?" I said.

Rodriguez stood. Z got up with him.

"We got an anonymous tip on a body, in a cave not far from where your business card was found," Rodriguez said. "Fortunately for you, your card wasn't found *in* the cave or we'd be talking downtown. If I discover, however, that any of you *were* in that cave, I come back with cuffs. And it won't be pretty. We understand each other?"

He looked around the room. No one spoke.

"Good." Rodriguez flicked a look toward the back of the room. He and Z filed toward the door.

"Detective."

Rodriguez turned. "Mr. Havens?"

"The body you found in the cave . . . was it a child?"

"Why do you ask?"

"I was thinking about a connection to the Wingate case."

Rodriguez tightened his lips and glanced at Z.

"Go ahead," she said. "They need to hear it."

The detective retraced his steps to the front of the room and leaned against the edge of Z's desk. One foot stayed on the floor; the other dangled. His hands were clasped elegantly in front of him.

"I know all about Skylar Wingate, Mr. Havens. He was taken almost fifteen years ago. In a homicide investigation, that's a lifetime. You understand what I'm saying?" Rodriguez didn't want or wait for an answer. "Evidence is the lifeblood of what we do. If you want me, or anyone else, to take you seriously, bring us some facts. Not a theory. Not a hunch. Not a coincidence. Hard, provable facts. Preferably ones that lead somewhere. Are we clear?"

We all nodded. Rodriguez didn't seem half satisfied but got up with a grunt and walked to the back of the room. Z led him out, the door slamming shut behind them. She returned in less than a minute. "I'm sorry that had to happen."

"It's not illegal to go into the woods," Havens said.

"And how were we to know there was a body there?" Sarah added.

I couldn't tell if my classmates were really angry or just blowing off steam after the cop left. Either way, Z didn't seem fazed in the least.

"Why did you run?" she said.

We gave a collective shrug.

"Why did you go in the first place?"

"Are you telling me you never did something similar?" Havens said.

"I didn't run when the police showed up," Z said. "Not if I had a right to be there." She dropped her voice a notch. "Now, tell me, please, you didn't go into that cave?"

"That was the first we've heard of it," I said.

Z searched our faces, each in turn, but found nothing.

"Who is he?" Sarah said. Z knew who Sarah was talking about. I thought Rodriguez might have that kind of effect on women. Regardless of circumstance.

"Rodriguez? Smart cop. Good guy. Honest."

"You mean they're not all honest?" I said.

"It's not a joke," Z said. "Maybe I should have told you this in our first class. If so, I apologize. But here it is. Don't screw with a Chicago cop. They can be ruthless, extremely violent, and largely devoid of conscience. If you threaten them, they'll do whatever they have to in order to protect themselves or whatever else they feel needs protecting. They carry a badge. They carry a gun. And some of them don't think twice before using either."

"I suspect we might have gotten a little taste of that already," Havens said. Then he described our trip to the evidence warehouse and my traffic stop.

"And you didn't feel the need to mention this when Rodriguez was here?" Z said.

"I don't remember him asking about it." Havens smiled. We all did. Except for Z.

"What did they get out of the car, Ian?"

"Paperwork from the Wingate file. Police reports, case notes. Stuff like that."

"And you kept no copies?" Z said.

"Those were the copies," Havens said, cutting me off. He didn't want Z to know about the notes I'd reconstructed from memory, which was fine by me.

"So you have nothing from the warehouse?" Z said.

"Hardly." That was Sarah. Hard to believe, but I'd almost forgotten about last night—the vodka, the beach, the swim.

"How so, Ms. Gold?"

"Big picture? Jake gets a letter about Wingate. We go to the crime scene and the police find another body nearby."

"You heard the detective. No plausible connection to Wingate."

"Still," Sarah said, "it happened. Fact. Then we go down to the warehouse, and all the evidence is gone. I mean, the box is there and a few scraps, but everything else is gone."

"Evidence often disappears," Z said. "Especially in older cases."

"Our point is this," Sarah said. "We think there's something wrong here." She paused. Havens and I nodded in agreement. "Someone doesn't want us to look at this case. And we don't understand why."

Z creased her upper lip with her knuckle and sank into a frown. I thought she might have forgotten we were there when she suddenly spoke. "How did you guys feel about my bringing in Rodriguez today?"

"I thought it sucked."

"Don't pull any punches on my behalf, Mr. Havens."

"How would you feel, if you were sitting in our seats?" Havens said.

"I'd probably feel like I got sandbagged."

"Exactly."

Z turned to me. "What do you think, Ian?"

"I think you struggled with the decision but thought Rodriguez was a homicide cop and it was better we talk here than downtown." I paused. "But I gotta agree with Jake. From where we sit, it sucked."

"Fair enough. The next question is this: Do you still trust me?"

"Do you trust us?" Sarah said.

Z tilted her head and narrowed her eyes. "I can't say I'm thrilled with what you've been up to. But I'm impressed. And a little intrigued."

"That's not an answer," Sarah said.

"I guess I'm going to have to think about it."

"Right back at you," Sarah said.

Z rocked lightly in her chair. I thought she might get up and leave. Suspend the seminar. Pull the next three students off her waiting list and start all over. I couldn't half blame her.

"You honestly don't think there's something wrong here?" Havens said.

"I can't tell you how many cases I've looked at, Mr. Havens, where I *knew* something was wrong. I knew it. But I couldn't prove it. The facts just weren't there. Sometimes they even pointed in an opposite direction. So I kept my mouth shut and watched the bad guys walk. Hardest part of the job, and a lesson you all need to learn. You heard Rodriguez. It's not what someone *did*. It's what you can *prove*."

"We need a little more time with Wingate," I said.

"You've had three days and nearly gotten arrested twice."

"That's not a problem," I said.

"For you, maybe not. For the university, it's a big problem."

"You still haven't told us what you think of the case," Havens said.

"I told you it was intriguing. Which means nothing. Based on what I've actually seen, your investigation is at a dead end."

"We still have a couple of leads to run down," I said.

"And you don't want to tell me about them?"

"We want you to trust us," Sarah said.

Z's fingers sounded like dead bolts as she drummed them on the desk. "Trust is a two-way street."

"We understand," Sarah said.

"I'm good with that," Havens said.

I just nodded.

"Okay. One more week." Z slipped on her glasses. "Right now, I need each of you to write up a memo on your trip to the forest preserve, as well as everything you remember about the evidence warehouse. Then I need a summary of where the investigation stands and what your next steps might be. Please give me as many specifics as you can spare."

"I've got a question," I said.

"Where would we be without it, Mr. Joyce?"

"The notes we generate in this class, could they wind up in the hands of your friend Rodriguez?"

"You mean voluntarily?"

"I mean at all."

"If the university should get subpoenaed, I would hope we would fight it as protected material under the First Amendment."

"You would hope?" Sarah said.

"No guarantees the school would fight. And certainly no guarantees we would win."

"How about you?" Havens said. "Would you turn our stuff over to the cops?"

"Are there any surprises in there?"

"That's not the answer we're looking for," Havens said.

Z sighed. "Provided you haven't broken any laws, I would, of course, keep any work product confidential. If I find something that's troubling, then we talk about it. Before anything goes anywhere. Fair enough?"

"Fair enough," I said. My classmates agreed.

"Okay," Z said. "Here's how it's going to work. If you get any leads, any hard evidence you think someone like Rodriguez might be interested in, you bring it to me. Immediately. Understood?"

We all nodded again. And, in doing so, promptly broke rule number one.

"Good. Get going on your memos." Z dismissed us with a wave and reached into the bottom drawer of her desk for some aspirin. She slugged them down with a Coke.

I opened my laptop and created a new document titled WINGATE INVESTIGATION. I snuck a look at my classmates. Sarah smiled back. Havens gave me a quick nod. We hadn't told Z about the two old cases we'd connected to Wingate for a simple reason. Sixteen years ago, she'd been the lead reporter on one of them: an inside look as investigators worked the disappearance of Billy Scranton. Havens shared the *Tribune* stories with us just before we walked into Z's class. It was good stuff. Good enough to win our professor her first Pulitzer.

Conflict of interest, indeed.

20

We walked out of Fisk at a little after eleven. The campus was ripe with summer. Lawns, thick and lush. Trees, dappled with touches of late-morning sun. Along the paths, flowers bloomed in rushes of color: pinks and blues, orange, lavender, and carpets of yellow. No one spoke as we walked. No one was anxious to break the spell. We passed through the university's main gate and stopped at the corner of Chicago Avenue and Sheridan Road. A lime-green VW rolled up to a red light. Z was behind the wheel. None of us said a word. The light changed, and she accelerated away.

"Nice color," Havens said. "Think it works with her hair?"

"Shut up." Sarah hit the button on the traffic signal. We waited for the light to change again and crossed the street.

"What did you think about Rodriguez?" I glanced across at my classmates.

"I thought we stuck up for ourselves pretty well," Havens said.

"I thought it was scary," Sarah said. "And I'm glad we didn't leave anything inside that cave."

"You think there's any chance the boy in the cave is connected to Skylar Wingate?" I said.

"We already talked about this," Havens said.

"Why did you ask Rodriguez about it?"

"Just to see if he agreed with us. And he did. Too much time between crimes. Unless we find evidence otherwise, end of story." Havens rubbed his belly and grumbled. "How about some lunch?"

We found his car parked illegally, with an NU parking ticket stuck on its windshield. "Fuck them." Havens threw the ticket in the gutter and popped the locks. "Get in."

"My car's up by Norris," Sarah said.

Havens waved her into the backseat. "I'll give you a lift."

Sarah's car was in a lot near the student center. She followed us back up Sheridan. I rode with Havens.

"Where are we going?" I said.

"Your choice," Havens said.

"Take a left on Central. About a mile up, there's a place called Mustard's Last Stand."

"Any good?"

"Oh, yeah."

Mustard's Last Stand had been a Northwestern staple for forty years. A red-roofed shack jammed next to Ryan Field, it specialized in dogs and Polish, 100 percent Vienna beef, shoestring fries, steamed buns, and all the fixings. Not bad before a football game. Or any other time for that matter. I tried to eat there at least twice a week.

We ordered at the counter. Our grill man was a guy named Smitty. He was from Glasgow. How a Scotsman wound up in Mustard's was an enduring mystery to everyone, especially Smitty. He'd worked there for five years. Mostly because he was too big to fire and no one could understand a thing he said anyway. Today, Smitty wore the standard uniform, a yellow Mustard's Last Stand T-shirt and a red bandana around his otherwise bald dome. He was sweating profusely and swatted at a bug that had crawled onto the white wax paper he wrapped the dogs in.

"Ian, how are ye?"

"Good, Smitty. How you doing?"

"I'm a wee bit fucked at the moment. One of the fryers is down and the cunt of a repairman was supposed to be here an hour ago."

"That sucks."

"I don't need it, Ian. Last night, I go for a few pints. Celtic are playing Barcelona in a friendly. Messi gets three and my boys get pounded. Fucking Spanish bastards."

"Next time, Smitty."

"Aye." He swatted at another small bug and flicked it away with the back of his hand. For the first time, he registered Sarah and smiled. "Ye brought some friends in."

Sarah had no idea, I was certain, what the Scotsman had been babbling about. And was appropriately horrified, I was also certain, at the swatting of flies, et cetera. No matter. Smitty loved pretty women. And so the Glasgow accent got that much thicker.

"And what might your name be, lassie?"

"Sarah Gold."

"Sarah Gold. Now isn't that just lovely. Are ye a friend of Ian's?"

"We go to Medill."

"Medill. How come I've never seen ye around here?"

"I usually come at night. After I've had a few beers."

"Aye, a good few pints never hurts." Smitty gave her his best Glasgow chuckle. He took her hand in his and looked like he was ready to settle in for a nice long chat. Meanwhile, the dog line was snaking out the door.

"Smitty," I said, "you got some people waiting."

He waved me away. "Them doggies aren't goin' anywhere, Ian. I see the little fuckers every day, and not one has ever jumped up and run down Central Street."

I pointed to myself and Jake. "We gotta get back to campus."

"We do," Sarah said.

The Scotsman reluctantly let go of her hand and straightened. Someone yelled about the hold up. Smitty was oblivious. "What can I get for ye?"

Jake and Sarah ordered the number one: a hot dog, fries, and a Coke. Jake got his with mustard. Sarah dragged hers through the garden. I spent the extra fifty cents and got a number two: a Polish, fries, and a Coke. Smitty piled on extra fries for Sarah. She promised she'd be back.

The outside tables were full, so we sat on a row of stools jammed up against a wall covered in Northwestern and Chicago sports memorabilia. I stared at a picture of the Wildcats' 1949 Rose Bowl squad. Havens got an *SI* cover of Mike Adamle scoring a touchdown for the Bears. Sarah, a picture of Bobby Hull with all his hair and phony teeth.

"Good fries," Havens said.

"Great fries." Sarah took a bite of her dog and dripped mustard and relish down her fingers. "Hot dog's good, too."

"Smitty wants to throw you over his shoulder and take you back to wherever he's from," Havens said.

"Scotland," I said. "Glasgow."

"I think he's cute," Sarah said.

"They have a little dug-out basement," I said. "You access it by lifting up a piece of the floor. Smitty likes to take his women down there. He lays out a blanket for them. Right between a sump pump and the rat traps."

"Gross," Sarah said. Havens chuckled. We all dove in to our food.

"What's our next step with Harrison?" I said between bites of my Polish.

"Z gave us a week," Sarah said. "From what I've seen, it's just not enough time."

"It might be enough," Havens said.

"You know something we don't?" I said.

"We've got a meeting Tuesday with the principal at Skylar Wingate's school. She wasn't working there when he disappeared, but she's going to introduce us to at least one teacher who was."

"A teacher who knew Skylar?" I said.

"This guy was his gym teacher," Havens said. "Skylar's last class on the day he disappeared. The cops were all over him as a suspect, but the guy came up clean."

"And what's he gonna tell us?" I said.

"I'm guessing we'll find out Tuesday." Havens had polished off his dog in three bites. Now he rolled up the wrapper and swished it into a barrel on the other side of the room.

"Nice shot," Smitty said.

Havens waved him off and turned back to me. "You don't like the school idea?"

"It's not that," I said.

"You got anything better, I'm listening."

"There's one other thing we should probably think about. I got it from the police reports we picked up in the evidence warehouse."

"One of the things you 'remembered'?" Havens said.

"Yeah. It was the address and phone number for the Street Ministry. And a couple of names."

"What's the Street Ministry?" Sarah said.

"It's a homeless shelter and soup kitchen," Havens said. "A couple of blocks from Skylar's school. James Harrison was living there at the time he was arrested."

"I was thinking I might check it out while you guys talk to the teacher," I said. "Two birds with one rock."

"One rock?" Havens said.

Sarah smiled. "Sounds good, Ian."

Havens seemed a little hacked off, probably because he hadn't thought of it. Or maybe because of the way Sarah called me Ian. Wishful thinking, perhaps, but it was my daydream, so what the hell. In the end, Havens rolled with the plan.

"I'll text you guys the address for the school. We're supposed to be there at nine-thirty." Havens turned to me. "Is it all right if I leave the files on the other two cases with you? My neighborhood's had a lot of break-ins this summer, and I don't want to lose the stuff."

"Sure."

The three of us walked out to his car and transferred Havens's Bankers Boxes to Sarah's trunk.

"I've got a couple more in my apartment," Havens said.

"You home tomorrow afternoon?" I said.

"Should be."

"Give me your address and I'll swing by."

Havens jotted down the address, then climbed into his car.

"Hold on," I said and put a hand on the door. "We should talk about Z."

"What is there to talk about?"

"She covered the Scranton case."

"More than covered," Sarah said. "She won the Pulitzer Prize for it."

"And knew everything that was going on inside the investigation," Havens said.

"What does that mean?" I said.

"Who knows? Maybe she was in the cops' hip pocket. Maybe when she realizes we suspect Wingate is connected to Scranton and they were both framed, she tries to screw us. Maybe she already knows and is screwing us as we speak."

"That what you think, Jake?"

"I don't know and I don't care. We've got our teeth into this thing. I say we take it where it goes, at least for another week. If Z gets herself fucked in the process, too bad." Havens trailed a hand out the window as he pulled away from the curb. "Have fun you two. See you tomorrow, Joyce."

He gave me an evil grin and was gone.

Sarah and I watched Havens's car disappear down Central. Then we began to walk.

"You think he's right?" I said. "About Z?"

"Probably not. But there's no reason to tell her everything either."

"She probably knows the Scranton murder as well as anyone. If there's something there, she might be able to see it."

"And then there's the other possibility," Sarah said.

"You think she'd screw around with us on this?"

"You're talking about a major milestone in her career, Ian. If our theory holds up and they arrested the wrong guy, it becomes a major embarrassment. Or worse."

We walked for a while, past a small group of stores and into another residential block. The houses here were nice, with wide driveways and watered lawns. A woman came out of a Prairie-style home carrying a stack of plastic chairs. She lined them up in a row at the corner of Lincolnwood, and disappeared back down the driveway. Next to her white chairs was a blue blanket and battered chaise longue. Across the street was a line of twenty folding chairs.

"What's up with all this?" Sarah said.

"All what?"

"The chairs on the sidewalk?"

"You've been in Evanston for how long?"

"Four years and counting."

"It's July first. People are putting out their chairs to reserve spots for the Fourth of July parade."

"Seriously?"

"Never been here for the summer?"

"No."

"People used to get crazy. Stake out spots two weeks in advance. Rope off areas. Now they have a law. July first and no sooner. By tomorrow Central will be covered in lawn chairs, beach chairs, blankets. I've seen whole living rooms out here."

"Folks love their parade, huh?"

"An American classic."

We'd drifted a mile or so down Central, into another commercial strip. There was a small park to our right.

"You want to sit?" I said.

"Sure."

We found a bench. People were taking their kids in and out of an Italian ice store across the street. We sat in the sun and let it warm our faces.

"I need some color," Sarah said.

I looked over. She had her eyes closed. Her skin was perfect.

"You look great," I said.

"Please."

"You're a beautiful woman, Sarah."

She shaded her eyes and stared at me. "Don't say that."

"Why not? It's true."

She sighed and stretched. Then dismissed me by closing her eyes again.

"What's up?" I said.

"Nothing."

"Tell me."

"You don't want to hear it."

"Fine."

We lapsed into silence until Sarah broke it.

"You want to know what I am, Ian?"

"From the sound of it, maybe not."

"I'm what they call 'almost good-looking.'"

"What the hell does that mean?"

"It means I'm not quite one of 'them,' but almost."

"Not quite one of who?"

"Never mind. You don't get it."

I got it. I just never met anyone who would actually acknowledge it. Never mind talk about it.

"You're one, Sarah. Hell, you define the category."

"That's sweet, Ian, but you're wrong. I'm almost one."

If Sarah Gold was in the "almost" category, I shuddered to think where I fell.

"Jake's one," she said. "You're a guy, but you can still see it. Looks, brains, probably played sports. I'm sure Mr. Havens has no trouble with women."

"Let's talk about something else."

Sarah opened her eyes and crinkled her nose. "Did I say something wrong?"

"No."

"I'm sorry."

"Don't be. You just told the truth."

"Sometimes that gets me in trouble."

"It's fine."

"You're a good-looking guy, Ian."

"Can we change the subject?"

"You are." She might have been smiling when she said it, but I was looking straight into the sun and couldn't tell.

"I'm thirsty," I said. "You want a drink or something?"

"Sure."

We went across the street and got a couple of lemonades at Food-stuffs. Then we sat at a table in the shade.

"What do you know about Jake?" she said.

"Jake again."

"I told you. I don't have a thing for him."

"It's okay if you do."

"I know it's okay, but I don't. I'm serious, Ian. What do you know about his family?" Sarah took a sip of her lemonade. I could feel her gaze prickle my skin.

"I'm not following you."

"Why do you think he's so into the Wingate case?"

"Because of the letter he got?"

"There's more to it than that." She pulled her chair closer until our foreheads were almost touching. Her words came out in a rush. "Jake had a younger brother who drowned back east. Cape Cod, I think. Have you heard this?"

I shook my head.

"Jake was ten or twelve, and his brother was, like, eight. They were diving off some rocks, and his brother got caught up in the ropes from some lobster pots. Jake's dad had told them not to swim there, but they did anyway. Jake dove down a bunch of times to try and save him. Instead, he watched his brother drown."

"Jake told you all this?"

"We went out for a few beers after we walked you home the other night."

"And why are you telling me?"

"I don't know. I guess Jake just seems really intense about Wingate."

"And you think that's because of his brother's death?"

"What do you think?"

"I think you should have asked him why he was the one who got the letter about Wingate. If maybe the person who sent it knew about his brother. Knew Jake would be vulnerable to that sort of thing."

"Is that what you believe?"

"Maybe." I looked out across Central. The sun was hard and bright in the middle of the street. A woman in jeans and a white top was yelling at her kid, who had wandered too close to the curb. We finished our drinks and walked some more. The conversation about Havens lay heavy between us. After a while we turned back down Central. By the time we got to Sarah's car, a breeze had sprung up. The air felt good on my skin.

"You headed home?" I said.

Sarah nodded. "Come on. I'll drop you off."

I sat in the front seat, with the flat of my foot up against the dashboard. Sarah didn't mind or I wouldn't have. A cut from *Exile on Main Street* came on the radio. "Shine a Light." She sang along with the lyrics.

"You like the Stones?" I said.

"I saw the movie. Scorsese."

"Get the album. *Exile on Main Street*. Listen to the whole thing."

Sarah saluted. "Yes, sir."

We pulled up to my house.

"Thanks for the lift," I said. "I'll see you Tuesday?"

"You want to ride together?"

"Sure."

"Good. I'll pick you up." She leaned over and gave me a dry kiss on the lips. A brother-and-sister kiss if there ever was one. Put our night on the beach to bed. I began to get out of the car. She touched my arm. "You gonna get those boxes out of my trunk?"

"I didn't forget."

"You want me to help you bring them in?"

"Let's just put them in my car for now."

We transferred Havens's Bankers Boxes to my backseat. Sarah sat up on the hood and swung her feet in the air. "Wednesday. The Fourth of July parade."

"What about it?" I said.

"Are you going?"

I never went to the parade. Then again, I wasn't entirely stupid either. "Never miss it. Why?"

"I was thinking it might be fun."

"You want to go?"

Sarah nodded. "If it's okay."

"It's okay."

"Great. What time?"

"I've got some things to do in the morning. Maybe around ten? We can get some breakfast and then head over."

"It's a date. You going over to Jake's apartment tomorrow?"

"I gotta pick up the rest of his files."

"Good."

"Why is that good?"

"I don't know. You guys seem to work well together. You click."

"What planet are you living on?"

"Do you really think someone sent Jake that letter because of his family?"

"If they wanted to hit a nerve, he's the guy. What does it matter? The case deserves to be looked at."

"You're right." Sarah slid off the hood and gave me another hug. "See you Tuesday."

I watched her car until it disappeared around the corner. Then I climbed into my own and picked through the material Jake Havens had collected. Sarah had assumed the boxes of evidence were going into my house. I'd learned a lesson, however, from my run-in with the Chicago police. So I took out my cell phone and made a call.

21

Jake Havens lived at the corner of Forty-sixth and Greenwood, in a South Side neighborhood called Kenwood. Like my classmate, the neighborhood was something of an enigma. Walk ten blocks in one direction and you'd find Barack Obama's Chicago home. Beyond that, the University of Chicago. A half mile the other way and stripped-down buildings stood naked in the sun. Boarded up. Vacant. Silent. Save for the cash-and-carry drug trade. And that went on 24/7.

It was almost four in the afternoon when I pulled up to Jake's building. There was a small park across the street named after the Chicago poet Gwendolyn Brooks. A couple of kids were playing hoops on an asphalt court, and a mom pushed a stroller along one of the park's sunlit walking paths. A mail carrier worked the far end of the block, and a shirtless man stood in the street, washing down his car with a hose and a sponge.

Havens lived on the second floor of a brick six-flat. I knocked on his door. It creaked open at first touch.

"Hello? Jake?"

I took a step inside and stopped. A dusty hallway stretched out in front of me. At the other end was a room with windows covered by heavy shades.

"Havens? You here?"

I walked tentatively down the hall and into what appeared to be a living room. There was a cheap sofa sitting on a threadbare rug and a couple of small round tables. On one of the tables was a framed photo of Jake as a boy. I picked it up. Jake was standing in a boat, smiling into the sun, and holding a largemouth bass that was half as long as he was. Sitting next to him was a younger boy, with a shock of flaxen hair and a face full of freckles. The younger kid looked up at Jake with a mixture of innocence and awe that would have broken my heart if I'd let it. I moved my eyes back to Jake. The strong jaw was there, the clear eyes, the certainty of who he was, the instinctive command of the moment. I wondered if this had been the trip. If this had been the summer. Jake at ten years old, diving into the cold salt water, following the lines of the lobster trap, watching his brother drown.

I put the picture down and ventured deeper into the apartment. A kitchen, draped in darkness, was set off to one side of a short hallway. On the other side, two doors. One was closed. The other stood open. A yellow light burned inside. I walked toward the light.

It was Havens's bedroom, except I wasn't sure where he slept. The bed itself was covered with paperwork from the investigation. Files carpeted the floor and ran in a row down one wall. Photos, sketches, and random notes were pinned to the walls, doors, furniture, and every other available bit of space. I pulled a piece of paper off Jake's headboard. It was a diagram of the interior of a building.

"The original's in one of the boxes I gave you."

I jumped in my skin and turned. Havens stood in the doorway, arms crossed, a crooked smile on his face.

"Hey." I sounded weak. Out of breath. "Your front door was open so I came in."

"'Coming in' means you walk in, see no one's around, and wait in the living room."

I felt my face burning but knew I wasn't going to back down. Not with Havens. "If you're waiting for an apology, it's gonna be a while."

He shook his head and snatched the diagram from my fingers. "You know what this is?"

"A mechanical drawing of some sort?"

"It's Skylar Wingate's grammar school."

"The place we're going to tomorrow?"

"The cops searched it from top to bottom after Skylar disappeared. They spent a day and a half right here." Havens pointed to a spot he'd circled in red. "In the boiler room."

"Why?" I said.

"Don't know, but they searched. So I'm gonna take a look."

"What makes you think there'll be anything left?"

Havens snapped his head up. "Left from what?"

I could feel his eyes on me. Fierce, intelligent, restless. "You're the one with the diagram, Jake. You tell me."

He folded up the drawing and slipped it into his pocket. "You're right. It's a long shot, but I figure it's worth a try."

I glanced past his shoulder, down the dim hallway. "You got a roommate?"

"He's gone for the Fourth. Lives in Columbus."

"And you sleep in here?"

Havens chuckled. "I call it the ugly brown room. I just push some papers off the bed and crawl in. I know, it's weird, but that's how I roll. College, law school, finals. I just sink into the stuff. Literally. And I don't surface until I get it right."

There was a large photo of Billy Scranton in his school uniform thumbtacked to the wall. I pulled it off and held it up. "And this stuff never bothers you?"

"You mean the murders?"

"The murders, the kids, the evidence. You don't mind all of it in your bedroom?"

"You get used to it. I've got a bunch more down here." Havens sorted through a pile on the floor and came up with an armful of folders.

"What are those?" I said.

"ViCAP pulled up eighteen more cases that might fit our pattern." Havens lined up the folders on his bed. Each file had a photo of a child clipped to its front.

"That's a lot of kids," I said.

"We'd have three times this amount if we asked for the ones whose bodies were never found."

"And you're telling me each of these is somehow connected to Skylar Wingate?"

"Didn't say that. These cases fit our general search parameters only. ViCAP runs each case through several more filters before spitting out a final list. Chances are none of these wind up fitting our specific pattern. Then again, we'll never know for sure."

"Why's that?"

"You want some coffee?"

"You gonna answer my question?"

"Let's get some coffee."

Ten minutes later, we were sitting in Havens's kitchen. I couldn't find any sign he ever used the place. No pots, pans, glasses, dishes. No food that I could see. Just a coffeemaker, a sack of beans, and a couple of mugs. We sat on stools under the pale light from an overhead fixture and finished off what was left of a pot of blended Sumatra.

"I went over to the law school this morning to do some follow-up on ViCAP," Havens said. "My professor told me my requests got kicked back."

"What does that mean?"

"It means someone's squeezing the information pipeline dry. I can't get additional data on any of the new cases. In fact, I couldn't even get into the system."

"How do you log on to ViCAP?"

A smirk flitted across his lips. "So you think so, too?"

"Think what?"

"We've hit another trip wire and the alarms are going off."

"How did you log on?"

"It was a general log on from the law school. They can't trace it back to me . . . or my professor."

"But they still shut things down?"

"My prof thinks they could have tagged sensitive files in ViCAP and triggered a shutdown if anyone made a request. Sort of a fail-safe to cover their ass."

"How much does your professor know about what we're doing?"

"Hardly anything. I'm not saying he's not interested, but I've kept him out of it."

We sipped at our coffees. In my mind, I pictured a virtual game of chess, except our chessboard was a graveyard and our pawns were dead kids.

"I don't think I can take all that stuff," I said.

"All what stuff?"

"Everything you've got in your room. What did you call it?"

"The ugly brown room."

"Right. Well, I can't store everything you've got in there. Hell, I couldn't fit it all in my car."

Havens shook his head. "No need. The new cases are useless without access to ViCAP. Everything else is mostly copies. I just have two more boxes I want you to take."

"Cool."

"You want 'em now?"

"Sure."

We walked back into the living room. I picked up the photo of Jake in the boat. It was the only scrap of personal life I could find in the entire apartment. "Nice fish," I said.

Jake took the photo from me and looked at it as if he'd forgotten who was in it.

"That your brother?" I said.

He nodded. "Sarah tell you about him?"

"A little. I'm sorry, Jake."

"It's all right. His name was Charley." Jake put the photo back on the table. "She tell you I was adopted?"

"No."

"Yeah. Nice people. Love 'em a lot."

"But?"

"But nothing." He shrugged. "It's just not the same."

I nodded toward the picture. "I never did stuff like that. And I had a real mom growing up."

"What's your point?"

"Just that."

"Just what?"

"Everyone's different. And everyone's got stuff they drag around."

"I'll write that down first chance I get." Havens jerked his head toward the hallway. "You want those boxes or not?"

He led me to a small utility closet. There were two more Bankers Boxes inside, sealed up and ready to roll. I saw a knife and duct tape on the floor beside them. We each took a box and walked down to my car, where we packed them away in the trunk.

"I'll see you tomorrow," I said.

"Wingate's grammar school. Nine-thirty. And don't be late."

I stuck out my hand. We shook, my grip disappearing into his.

"I'm sorry about earlier," Havens said, his voice drifting off into a soft mumble.

"Don't be."

"Bullshit. That was an asshole thing to say. I love my family. And I'm lucky to have them."

"Yeah, you probably are."

"See you tomorrow, Joyce."

"Sure." I climbed into my car and started down the block. In my rearview mirror, Havens stood in the street, hands on his hips, and watched me go.

22

Skylar Wingate's grammar school was on the Northwest Side of the city. It was housed in a redbrick building and flanked on one side by a cement playground. Sarah and I got there at nine-fifteen. Havens was sitting on the front steps, waiting for us.

"You guys see the papers this morning?" he said.

"I don't read the newspaper," Sarah said.

"Online?"

"Oh, no, I didn't get a chance."

"How about you, Joyce?"

"I scrolled through a few things."

"Our pal Rodriguez was in the news."

"Why?"

"Police finally issued a statement about the body they found in the cave. I thought the press would give it more play, but the kid was a runaway."

"Which means no one gives a damn?" Sarah said.

"John Wayne Gacy killed thirty-three kids," Havens said. "To this day a bunch of them have never been ID'd."

"So?" Sarah said.

"So, do you give a damn?"

"I didn't know . . ."

"Exactly. You didn't know." Havens dismissed the subject with a wave of his hand. Sarah looked like she might take a swing at him.

"Maybe we should focus on today," I said and pointed to the school's run of flat glass windows, curtains drawn down tight. "Where are all the kids?"

"Summer vacation," Havens said. "Place will be a ghost town until fall."

"And where was Skylar last seen?"

Havens pointed to the far end of the playground. "He walked out of that gate down there."

"That's where I'm headed."

"You sure you don't want to come in?" Havens said. "Talk to this guy?"

I shook my head. "You two talk. I'll be back in an hour or so."

Havens stood up and headed toward the school's front door. Sarah gave him a sour look as he went past, wiggled her fingers at me, and followed. I waited until they'd disappeared inside. Then I took out my smartphone and pulled up the news on Rodriguez's presser. I scrolled through the stories but couldn't find the name of the victim in the cave or any details on leads. I logged off and listened. In the hush of the school yard, I could hear their voices. The dry whispers of dead children scratching in the shadows.

I walked the length of the playground and stepped through the gate. The homes here were much like those in Evanston, set back from the street, with big yards, long driveways, and tall rows of hedges. Birds chirped at me from the trees. Kids yelled and played. I came up to the crosswalk at Peterson Avenue. Traffic streamed past in both directions. Skylar Wingate would have stopped here and made a choice. He could turn left and walk a couple of commercial blocks before circling back to his own. Or he could stick to the side streets and take the long way home. The police had theorized Skylar took the shortcut—one that took him within hailing distance of the Street Ministry.

I hit the button and waited for the walk signal. Then I crossed Peterson and turned left.

The ministry was housed in a white frame building, with an adult bookstore on one side and a liquor store on the other. It was still early in the morning, and the crowd outside was sparse. Just a boy and girl in their early twenties, tattooed and pierced, sitting with their backs against the building. The boy was the more ragged of the two. He saw me and put his hand out. I found three dollars in my pocket and gave them to him. That seemed to get the girl's attention. She was Latina, dark hair streaked with gold, eyes trimmed in brown, and a full, generous mouth. It was a face that was hard around the edges, one that would grow old quickly.

I heard a noise and glanced at her hands, folded in her lap. She opened them. There was a small brown-and-white pigeon there. I stepped back, but it just stared at me.

"Yours?" I said.

The girl made a small gesture, and the bird flew off. "You looking for someone?" she said.

I nodded at the building and gave her a name. She shook her head. I gave her another. She stood and motioned for me to follow. The girl was smaller than I thought, with strong shoulders. She moved like an athlete.

Inside, there was a long counter with cubbyholes behind it filled with bags, boxes, and cans of food. The girl pointed to a row of folding chairs and disappeared through a doorway. I sat and waited. Five minutes later, a black woman came out. She was in her mid-sixties, thin, with fine features marred by a jagged scar that started at her lower lip and ended in the cleft of her chin. She gave me a firm, dry handshake and looked me straight in the eye.

"My name's Grace Washington. I run the shelter."

"Ian Joyce. I'm a grad student at Medill."

Grace nodded as if that was entirely expected. "What can I do for you, Ian?"

"I'm working on a story. Actually, it's something that happened quite a while ago." My eyes drifted to the doorway behind her.

"Would you like to discuss this in my office?" Grace said.

"That would be great."

We walked down a short hallway to a small room with a desk, chair, and filing cabinet. I sat. Grace closed the door and took her place behind the desk.

"How can I help you, Ian?"

I took out the notes I'd made on James Harrison and held them in my lap. "It's about a murder, ma'am."

Grace arched an eyebrow but didn't respond.

"In 1998 one of your clients, a man named James Harrison, was convicted of killing a local boy. Skylar Wingate."

"I knew James."

"I know. Your name was in one of the police files."

"I see."

I shuffled my notes in my hands. "I'm in a seminar where we take a look at old cases."

"Cases where you think the convicted man might be innocent?"

"Exactly."

"And you want to take up James's case?"

"That's why I'm here."

"You know James is long past caring whether he was innocent or guilty? They killed him in his cell."

"I know, but if he was innocent, we think it should be looked at."

"That's what you think?"

"Yes, ma'am."

"How many convicted killers have you met, Ian?"

"None."

"Uh-huh. You know about the DNA? The match to James's pants?"

"We think it doesn't make sense."

"Why?"

I shrugged. "I can't tell you everything, Ms. Washington, but it just doesn't."

"Sounds like you think you know something the rest of us don't." She sharpened her eyes a touch, but I kept my mouth shut.

"All right, Ian. What is it you want?"

"What did you talk to the police about?"

"Nothing. They came in, wanted to see where James slept, poked around for a while, and left."

"Did they take anything with them?"

"This all happened years ago."

"Are you telling me you don't remember?"

"They took everything James owned, which wasn't much."

"Did they ask you any questions?"

"I don't think they were very interested in asking questions."

"Do you think James did it?"

"Not a chance in hell."

"Did you think he did it at the time?"

"No."

"What about the DNA?"

Grace got up from her chair, walked over to the filing cabinet, and came back with a thick folder. She opened it and gave a soft sigh of surprise.

"What is it?" I said.

"Nothing." She took a photo out of the folder. "You ever see a picture of James?"

"Only his mug shot."

She slid the picture across. It was taken on a sunny day, in front of the ministry. James Harrison was sitting on the curb, elbows on his knees, the butt of a cigarette caught between forefinger and thumb. He had skin the color of beaten copper, with sharp cheekbones and dark eyes shot through with jaundice.

"How old was he?" I said.

"That was taken maybe a year before he was arrested. I'd say he was around thirty, thirty-two."

"Looks awfully skinny."

"When he wasn't drunk, James was a junkie. Lived on the streets for eight years." Grace slid the picture back into the folder. "He was a regular here. Nothing special. Just a sweet man. Quiet."

"Not the kind to kidnap a kid off the street and kill him?"

"James was more likely to be killed himself. Just had that sort of luck. You asked about the DNA?"

"Yes."

"The police claimed to have found that boy's blood on a pair of James's jeans."

"And?"

"First of all, the witness who said he saw James with the boy. Wearing those jeans."

"Robert Atkinson?"

"Right, Bobby Atkinson." Grace shook her head at the name. "Junkie."

"Like Harrison?"

"Hardly. Atkinson would say anything the police wanted him to say."

"So you think he was lying?"

"Maybe not out-and-out lying, but Bobby wasn't the most reliable guy. He'd give you half a story and let you fill in the rest. Then swear up and down that's how it happened."

"Where's Atkinson now?"

"Dead." Grace held up her folder. "And then there's this."

She slid the folder across the desk. Inside I found a stack of papers stapled together. At the top of the cover page was the Street Ministry's name and MAY—JUNE—JULY 1998 printed in block letters.

"That's the inventory log we keep for our clothing and food supplies," Grace said. "We record what we take in here." She opened the log and pointed to one set of numbers, then flipped to another page and showed me a second. "And what we give out here."

I scanned the log. Each day had its own page. Grace directed me to the entries for June 6, 1998.

"This was two days before the Wingate boy disappeared. You see we had a pair of Wrangler jeans, size thirty-two, with a hole in the left knee and a rip in the back pocket."

I looked up at her and waited.

"I gave those jeans to James on May twenty-eighth. He wore them for a few days and gave them back. Didn't fit. 'Falling off me,' he said. That's when I logged them back in as inventory."

"On the sixth?"

"Yes."

"So what?"

"Those are the jeans the police claimed James was wearing on June eighth—the day he's supposed to have killed that boy."

"The jeans they pulled the victim's blood off of?"

Grace nodded.

"How do you know they're the same jeans?"

"I had stitched up the back pocket with red thread. James saw the jeans in court and said the stitching was exactly the same. Said they had a hole in the knee as well."

"When did you talk to James?"

"They kept him at Twenty-sixth and Cal during his trial."

"So you two were friends?"

"He had his demons, but James was a good man."

"You have a picture of the jeans?"

"No."

"You ever see them yourself? After James was arrested?"

"I didn't go down to the trial. Couldn't take it." Grace took the log in her hands and flipped ahead a few more pages. "We did a store inventory on June fifteenth. The jeans were still here. Did another at the end of the month." She turned the log around again so I could see. "The jeans were gone."

"And you have no record of having given them out?"

Grace shook her head. "Check for yourself."

"I believe you," I said and began to flip back through the pages anyway. "So you think someone came in here, took the jeans, and then used them at his trial to frame Harrison."

"A rip in one knee. Red stitching in the back pocket. How many jeans exactly like that?"

"If they're going to frame him, why not just get any old pair of jeans? Why come here?"

Grace looked around at the empty corners of her office. "The ministry's full of snitches. Sell their mother for a fix, a couple of bucks. Hell, they'd do it just for fun."

"So the cops wouldn't have a problem getting a pair of jeans out of your inventory if they wanted to? And if they knew they'd once belonged to James?"

"His DNA would be all over them, right?"

I shrugged. "It's not James's DNA that's the problem. It's the victim's."

Grace reached for her log. I held up a hand.

"I didn't say I didn't believe you. But we need to look at the hard parts of this as well. Any idea what James might have actually been wearing when he was arrested?"

"I know exactly. Green surgical scrubs. Had them on three days straight. Told me they made him feel like a doctor."

"I suppose James never saw the scrubs again after he was arrested?"

"Detectives claimed they arrested him wearing the jeans. James told me it fit with Atkinson's statement."

I made a few more notes and flipped the inventory log shut. "Did you ever go to the police with any of this?"

"Hell, yes. Police, prosecutor, alderman, newspapers. No one cared. No one believed me."

"How did the DNA testing come about?"

"James insisted on it. Minute the trial was over, that's all he talked about. 'Course he had no money."

"Let me guess, you lent him some?"

"We raised a little bit, but I'm not sure where he got the rest."

"Who was James's attorney on appeal?"

"Best I could tell he was doing it himself. You know about his attorney at trial?"

"Seemed pretty useless."

Grace rolled her eyes and snorted.

"Can I make a copy of this?" I said and put a hand on the log. Grace got up from behind the desk. "We have a copier in the back, if you want to wait. June and July of 1998?"

"May and August as well."

Grace nodded and left. I wandered back to the front. The Latina was behind the counter, stacking cans of tomato sauce.

"What happened to your pigeon?" I said.

She looked at me, shrugged, and went back to her cans. A middle-aged woman came in with a basket. The girl helped her fill it with food. The woman thanked her and left.

"Are you waiting for Grace?" the girl said.

"Yes."

"You can sit down if you want." She pulled out one of the folding chairs, and I sat on it.

"My name's Theresa."

"Hi, Theresa."

"Are you a student?"

"I'm a grad student at Northwestern," I said.

"I'd love to go there."

"Why don't you?"

She rolled her eyes and ran a hand through her hair. "Just got it done. What do you think?"

"It looks nice," I said.

"I want to be on TV. A newscaster."

"I'd say you got a shot."

She hooded her eyes and frowned. "Why do you say that?"

"I don't know."

"Maybe I'm stupid."

I was about to say, *Maybe you are,* but was just smart enough not to.

"You thought I was one of the junkies when you saw me outside. Like that guy I was with."

I shook my head, even though she was exactly right. "I didn't think anything."

She turned away in another pout as Grace came back into the room.

"Theresa, they're unloading some supplies in the alley," Grace said. "Why don't you go check them in."

The girl left without giving either of us another look. Grace sighed and turned back to me.

"Here are your copies. I hope they help."

"Thanks, Grace. Would you mind . . ."

She cut me off. "I've attached a business card. Anything else you need, give me a call."

We shook hands and walked to the front door. She stopped me with a light touch on the arm.

"One more thing, Ian." She took a look around to make sure we were alone. "This is Chicago we're talking about. Cops, detectives, prosecutors. I know you're a smart young man . . ."

"Are you suggesting I drop this?"

"I didn't say that. Not at all. Just tread lightly."

"I will." I held up the pages she'd copied. "Could you answer one more question for me?"

"If I can."

"This inventory log's fourteen years old. You want to tell me why you kept it?"

"James was a friend. But if he'd killed that boy, I would have said he got what he deserved. He didn't do it. And he didn't deserve to die the way he did."

"Thanks, Grace."

"Good luck." She opened the door and closed it behind me. I walked past the alley where they were unloading supplies. Theresa was there, directing traffic and flashing her dark, unreadable eyes. I kept walking, turning my thoughts to the jeans and Grace's theory. Even if there was something to it, I didn't see how we could prove anything. Not without the jeans themselves. It was like everything else we came across. A lot of speculation and precious little fact.

I crossed over Peterson. A half block from the grammar school I stopped. Jake and Sarah were sitting together on the front steps. He reached up and touched the side of her face. She pushed his hand away. Her laughter floated my way on a summer breeze. I walked through the small gate and across the playground. They both saw me at the same time.

"Joyce, how did you do?"

Havens was grinning and didn't seem the least bit uncomfortable.

I searched Sarah's face and found a small bit of unease. She knew I'd seen something. I just had no idea what.

"I did all right," I said. "How about you guys?"

Sarah patted the step beside her. "Sit down and we'll tell you."

I looked up at the school's green metal doors and shook my head. "Let's find someplace where we can spread out." I showed them the Street Ministry log. "Got some new information we need to look at."

We decided to head back to Northwestern and found a table at the Starbucks in Norris, universally known on campus as Norbucks. Havens went up to get some coffee. I took out the ministry log.

"What's that?" Sarah said.

"I'll tell you when Havens gets back."

"We still on for tomorrow?"

"The Fourth? You bet."

Havens returned with his coffee and took a seat. "Take their time up there."

"That's Norbucks," Sarah said. "Line. No line. They move at their own speed."

Havens took a sip and grimaced. "Awful." He stirred in three packets of sugar and took another sip. "Better."

"What did you find out at the school?" I said.

Havens put his coffee to one side and pulled his chair in close. "We talked to William Bryson. Skylar's gym teacher. He told us Skylar was nothing special. Nice, quiet. Just another student."

"Anything else?" I said.

"The police talked to Bryson," Sarah said. She'd taken out a legal pad and was looking at some notes. "He gave them a statement. Told them he didn't see Skylar outside of class that day. Didn't speak with him. Never saw him with anyone suspicious in or near the school. Never saw anyone suspicious hanging around." Sarah closed up her pad. "A whole lot of nothing."

"Is there anyone else at the school who was there when Skylar was killed?" I said.

"According to Bryson, he's the only one left," Sarah said. "The school board ordered some cutbacks a few years ago and bought out a bunch of people."

"I stuck my head in the furnace room," Havens said.

"And?"

"They put in a new system three years ago. Reconfigured the entire space."

"So the school's a washout," I said.

"I'm gonna go back in a day or two," Havens said. "Maybe have another talk with Bryson."

"Why?"

"I'm a detail guy. Sometimes people remember things after you give them a little time." Havens nodded toward the ministry log. "Now tell us about this."

I told them about the inventory. The jeans. And Grace. When I was finished, I sat back and waited.

"So Grace thinks the cops stole a pair of Harrison's jeans from her inventory and planted the victim's blood on them?" Sarah said.

"The jeans came in as evidence at trial," I said, "but only as to blood type."

"And Harrison paid for his own DNA testing on appeal, which would have confirmed his conviction if he'd lived?"

"That's right. Came back a hundred percent belonging to Skylar."

"Do you believe her?" Havens said.

"Grace? Yeah, I do. At least I believe she thinks she's telling me the truth."

"If she's telling the truth, it might explain why they'd want to get rid of all the physical evidence," Havens said.

Sarah nodded at my pile of notes. "You remember seeing anything in the evidence warehouse about what Harrison was wearing the night he was arrested?"

I shook my head. "That doesn't mean there wasn't a report filed."

"Of course there was a report filed," Havens said. "And they would have changed it to show he was wearing jeans. We're not going to find anything there."

I was about to respond when my phone buzzed. It was Grace.

"Mr. Joyce?"

"Hi, Grace." I glanced at Sarah, then Havens, who toasted the call with his cup of Norbucks.

"What's up?" I said.

"There was one thing I forgot to mention."

"Okay."

"When James had his DNA testing done, I wrote down the name of the scientist. He was a very nice man and did the work for a fraction of what it cost anywhere else."

"Did he think James was innocent?"

"He did. Until the test results came back. Anyway, I don't know if he's worth talking to. You probably already have his name."

I motioned for a pen and paper. Sarah slid both across the table.

"Actually, I don't have his name. Why don't you give it to me?"

"It's Sam Moncata. He used to work for the FBI. Now I guess he's on his own. Very nice man."

I nodded and scribbled. Grace gave me Moncata's address and the last phone number she had. I thanked her and was about to hang up when I thought of something.

"Grace, have you kept in touch with Mr. Moncata?"

"I haven't spoken to him in years."

"Oh."

"Why do you ask?"

"Well, if we show up at this guy's door out of the blue, asking about an old murder . . ."

"If it will help, you can tell him you talked to me. He'll remember."

"Thanks, Grace."

"Good-bye, Ian."

I hung up.

"What is it?" Havens said.

"Grace at the Street Ministry. She remembered the name of the guy who did the DNA testing for Harrison."

"That's the last guy we need to talk to," Sarah said.

"Wrong," Havens said. "First of all, our job is to find out the truth, right?"

"So now you think Harrison's guilty?" Sarah said.

"I think we're gonna need to find a hole in that DNA match sooner or later. If this guy made a mistake, maybe we can sniff it out. He also might have gotten a look at the jeans."

I sat up in my chair. "You think he has them?"

"I doubt it. Still, he's worth talking to. Besides, what else have we got? I say give him a call."

I did. Moncata was on his way out the door. I told him we were students. That didn't get him very excited. Then I mentioned the name James Harrison. And then Grace. Moncata said he could give us an hour. After the holiday. I hung up.

"He'll see us on the fifth. In the afternoon."

"Where is he?" Havens said.

"Downtown. Just off Michigan Avenue."

Sarah shook her head. "I've got some stuff to do that day for Omega."

"What's Omega?" Havens said.

"It's a crisis group for women. I volunteer there."

I wasn't sure why, but it pleased me to no end that Sarah hadn't told Havens about her work at the shelter. Even better, she had told me.

"That's cool," I said. "We'll meet with Moncata and fill you in later."

"Sounds like a plan." Havens zipped up his backpack and slung it over his shoulder. "What are you guys doing for the Fourth?"

"Going to the parade," Sarah said. There was an uncomfortable pause I was more than comfortable with. Sarah, unfortunately, was not. "You want to come?"

"Can't," Havens said. "Maybe later for a drink?"

Sarah smiled. I sulked the entire way home.

23

Over the years, he'd reduced the whole thing to an art form. Long walks, looping in and out of neighborhoods, identifying patterns, trolling for victims. Usually, he was hunting children. Ones who didn't fit in. Ones who needed a friend. Today, however, was different. Today he was simply looking for a way in.

The green-and-white house appeared to be all its age in the morning light. On his third pass down the block, he saw the boy leave and noted three men in a black sedan at the corner. The men made their move fifteen minutes later. They forced the front door, stayed for almost an hour, and came out the way they went in. That was four hours ago. Now he approached the house and pushed at the door. It creaked open. His nostrils quivered. The smell of stale fear permeated the space. He wandered through the first floor, stopping here and there to touch something. They'd done a thorough job of searching the place. And hadn't tried to hide it. He made his way down a hallway. The door to the basement was still locked. He forced it open and walked down the steps. The long, thick table was sleeping under a layer of dust. He wanted to take off his gloves and feel its surface, but couldn't. Instead, he dropped to his hands and knees in a corner and felt along the floor for a seam. Then he took out a flat bar and began to work. Three minutes later, he'd pried up a foot-square block of cement. He plunged his hand into the dark hole, but it was empty.

The man with the yellow eyes cursed. A single word that rang off the brick walls. A car pulled up outside with a squeak of springs. The man fitted the square of cement back into the floor and filled in the seams with dirt. Then he slipped into the backyard and worked his way around the block.

The boy was just getting out of the car. There was a girl behind the wheel. The same one from the lake. The boy carried himself like a man, but he wasn't. Not yet. Maybe never. The girl pulled away from the curb. She cruised past the man with yellow eyes, barely aware he was there. He committed her tag number to memory. Then he watched the boy walk up the path to his front door. By the time the boy turned around, the man was gone.

24

I stared at the open door for what seemed like a day and a half, then spun around and took a look behind me. Sarah was gone. The sidewalk was empty. I thought about calling the Evanston cops but decided to go inside instead. I got a baseball bat out of my front closet and walked into the living room. They hadn't trashed the place. Just moved around enough things so I knew they'd been there. I checked the kitchen, then went upstairs. My mom's bedroom was halfway down the hall. I hadn't been in it since she'd passed. Now I pushed open the door. Her clothes still stood on hangers in the closet. A hairbrush, some pictures of me, and her jewelry were arranged on the dresser. The checkered band of a Chicago police hat lay in the middle of her bed. I picked up the band and sat with it, wondering how long they'd been here, what they'd touched. I walked back downstairs. The basement door stood ajar. In the cellar, I crouched over the sealed-up hole in the floor. There were fresh chisel marks on the smooth stone. I walked across the room and removed a piece of paneling up high on the wall. Behind it was a camera with a pinhole lens and a portable recorder. I took out the recorder's memory chip and slipped it into my pocket. Then I went back upstairs and called a locksmith. After that I made a second call.

—————

Smitty met me in the dirt parking lot behind Mustard's.

"What are ye all about, Ian?"

"Nothing, Smitty."

He shielded his eyes with his hand and blinked against the sun. "You sure?"

"Yeah."

"Someone kicked in your door, Ian. Why aren't you calling the coppers?"

"Be better if I don't. Can I get my stuff?"

Smitty gave me another hard look, then led me inside, to a small kitchen prep area. He grabbed a handle screwed into the planked flooring and pulled. A section of the floor swung up, revealing a short flight of stairs. We went down, Smitty first.

"Watch your head," he said and snapped on a light. The basement was maybe a hundred feet square, the ceiling, barely six feet high. Havens's boxes were stacked along one wall, between cartons of frying oil and a reach-in cooler.

"You want to take them out of here?" Smitty said.

"Just a few things."

"Turn out the light when you're done."

Smitty left, and I was alone with the ViCAP files. Everything seemed to be in order. I pulled out the bite-mark photos Havens had shown me, along with a handful of supporting documents. Then I turned out the light. Upstairs, I ordered a dog and fries. I sat at a table outside, ate my dinner, and watched the traffic breeze past. The band from the cop's hat lay on the table in front of me. Along with the photos and the memory chip from my camera. It was the third of July. I was being watched. And I needed to figure out why.

25

A guard tugged open the gates to Calvary Cemetery and waved me in. I waved back and pulled into an empty parking lot. The Fourth had started out overcast, with gusts of rain blowing in off the lake. I locked my car and took a walk among the headstones. Calvary was the oldest existing Catholic cemetery in Chicagoland, and I was in the oldest part of it. To my left a statue of an angel looked down, arms spread, face rubbed smooth by the passage of time. Beneath the angel, I found the grave of Kevin Barry Byrne, dead in 1866. Next to Kevin was a large stone with a single line chiseled on it.

1804–1860 LOST ON LADY ELGIN

I'd done my homework from the last time I was here. The *Lady Elgin* was a side-wheel wooden steamship that was rammed by a schooner during a storm on Lake Michigan. More than three hundred people died, many of the bodies washing up on the rocks near Northwestern's campus. People don't think they can learn much in a cemetery, but there you go.

I walked past the marker for *Lady Elgin*'s nameless victim and came face-to-face with a young boy. He was maybe three feet tall and hewn out of white marble. The boy stood in a small black box with a glass face. The hinges and handle on the box were made of metal and green with age. The boy was frowning at me, wondering what I was doing here with the dead. I tickled my fingers across the top of the box and walked on.

My brother was where he always was. Under a tree, with a peek at Lake Michigan when it wasn't cloudy. I took out a tight bunch of flowers and put them on his grave. Then I sat on the grass and stared at his headstone.

MATTHEW JOYCE
FEBRUARY 6, 1990–JULY 4, 2000

I edged a finger into the cuttings on the stone and searched for the right feeling. But there were only the clouds and the smell of rain. The dirt and the grass. And my brother's remains, moldering in a box below me. So I stopped trying. And the tears came. Hot and wet like always. When they stopped, it was just as quick. And just as mysterious. I wiped my face and wondered if it would always be like this. It wasn't that I couldn't handle it. I handled it just fine, thank you.

I stayed at the grave for almost an hour. I didn't see another soul the entire time. Except for a coyote, looking for his breakfast. He was gray with a swatch of brown over his shoulders and down his back. I watched him until he started watching me. Then I turned away. When I looked back, he was gone.

I was threading my way back to the parking lot when I heard a footfall. It was a woman, maybe thirty yards away, bundled up against the weather and walking away from me on a path to my left. Something seemed familiar. Was it the cut of her coat? Maybe a flash of color? I turned for a second look, but the woman had disappeared. In the parking lot, two cars had joined mine. One was a beat-up red Toyota. The other, Z's lime-green VW. I crept into the graveyard again, careful this time not to make a sound.

I found her in the poorest section of Calvary, hard by the exhaust and noise from Chicago Avenue. I knew the section well because Matthew almost wound up there. Until my mom found some cash. And Matthew slept where he slept.

Z was dressed in black, a wisp of a hat riding atop her mop of red hair. She stood ramrod straight, hands clasped in front of her, and stared at a small patch of ground. I watched her lips move as she prayed and ducked behind a tree when she blessed herself. She knelt and placed something on the ground, blessed herself again, and got up to go. I waited, then walked over to the plot she'd been standing before. Z had placed a set of black rosary beads beside the grave marker. I left the beads where they were and jotted down the name carved in the rock. When I got back to the parking lot, Z's VW was gone. I started up my car and followed suit.

26

By the time I got home from Calvary, the skies had cleared and the day was beginning to heat up. Even better, Sarah Gold sat on my front steps.

"You're early," I said.

"It's my first parade. I'm excited."

"What do you got there?" I pointed to a white bag by her feet.

Sarah pulled out a handful of silver tubes. "What do you think?"

"What is it?"

"Face paint. Red, white, and blue."

"Not happening."

"It's the Fourth of July."

I shook my head. Sarah already had a tube of red open and a tube of blue. She smeared a couple of fingers worth down both sides of her face.

"I live here, Sarah."

"It will be fun." She handed me the tube of red. "Please?"

I squirted a little on my finger and wondered what I'd gotten myself into. Maybe it was just what I needed.

A half hour later, we were standing in front of a diner on Central called Prairie Joe's. They sat us at a table outside. Sarah ordered the huevos rancheros. I got scrambled eggs. Our orders were served with warm tortillas and coffee. By the time we finished, it was almost eleven, and the street was filling up with life. We walked for a bit and drank it in. Parents carrying cups of Starbucks and pushing strollers. Kids in baseball caps. Ice cream. Balloons. Flags. And face paint. I'd agreed to turn myself into a red, white, and blue fool, but only once the parade actually started.

We stopped at an antiques shop where Sarah looked at an old set of silver and a wooden box of some sort. Then we walked next door to the Spice House. I'd never been in the Spice House and, apparently, with good reason. The moment I walked through the door, I started sneezing.

"You all right?"

I shook my head and retreated to a bench outside.

"What's in there?" I said.

"Spices."

"What kind of spices?"

"Well, the sign says they have eight different kinds of paprika."

"Great."

I stayed on the bench while Sarah perused the stores of paprika, pepper, and whatever else they ground up inside the god-awful place. She came out with a small bag she kept at a careful distance.

"Sorry about that," she said.

"What did you get?"

"Cumin, red pepper, and chili powder. Good for tacos."

We walked some more. The sun was bright and hot now. A trombone had fired up somewhere, and the parade started. I bought us some ice cream. People smiled at us. Mostly because of Sarah, but I smiled back anyway. She linked her arm in mine and whispered in my ear.

"Time for the face paint."

I laughed and let her smear my face with streaks of color. Then I did the same to her. After that, we painted the faces of a couple of kids whose parents weren't around. We watched the parade go by. Yelled and cheered at the Evanston Marching Kazoo Band. Then some cops and firemen. Uncle Sam on a high two-wheeled bicycle did crazy circles around the parade mascot, Sparky the Firecracker. Kids floated by on floats. Old people rode past in cars that were even older. The governor of Illinois stopped to shake my hand. Best I could tell, he wasn't even wearing a monitoring bracelet.

We watched for two hours and got sunburned until someone gave us some sunscreen. Then we headed down the block to a bar called Clarence's. It had an outdoor patio that was filled with parade people. We found a table, and I went up to get a couple of beers. Sarah drank half of hers in one go.

"Fun?" I said.

"Wonderful." She clinked her nearly empty glass into mine. "Thank you very much."

"You don't go to parades in Michigan?"

"Charlevoix has a parade. We usually watch it from our boat."

"Nice."

"Not really. You sit out there all day with the same seven people."

"I guess it would be all right if it were the right seven people?"

"I guess. You want another one?"

"Sure."

Sarah started to get up, but a waitress was nearby and took her order. Sarah sat back down. We'd wiped off the face paint, but a handful of guys at the bar couldn't keep their eyes off her anyway. She was wearing shorts, a yellow tank top, and oversize sunglasses. With her hair pulled back and the glow from her day in the sun, I couldn't blame them.

"What?" Sarah slid the glasses up on her forehead.

"Huh?"

"You're sitting there, smiling."

"Can't I smile?"

"It's just that you don't do it that often."

"Do what?"

"Smile." She broke out a killer as the waitress put down our second round of beers. "It looks good on you, Ian. The smile, that is."

"You think so?"

"I do."

The beer was cold. Sarah insisted we clink glasses again. She giggled and slid her eyes over my shoulder, toward her admirers at the bar.

"They've been ogling you since we got here," I said.

She put down her beer and leaned close until our lips were almost touching. "Want to give them something to talk about?"

"I thought we were friends?" I said.

"We are." She eased back in her chair and took another sip from her pint. "Actually, I was worried about you this morning."

"Why?"

"You got out of your car like a black cloud. Grim."

"Sorry."

She waved her hands around us. "It's the summer. A parade. We're young and drinking beer. How bad can that be?"

"You're right."

"I know I'm right. So why?"

"Don't mess around, Sarah."

She slipped her hands over mine. They were warm and strong.

"I'm not messing around, Ian. If you have a problem, I'd like to think I can help."

"It's not a problem."

"Then what is it?"

Maybe it was the beer. Maybe it was her. Maybe it was just the need to feel something more. Something I could hang on to. Whatever it was, it opened the door. And I walked through.

"I visited a graveyard this morning."

She didn't expect that. Probably wished she'd just drunk her beer and kept her mouth shut. But now she was in for it. And so it went.

"Why?"

"I had a twin brother, Matthew. He died when he was ten. Today's the anniversary."

"I'm so sorry."

It was the second time she was sorry for me. And I still hated it.

"Let's just forget about it."

"No."

"Yes. It was a long time ago, and I paid my respects this morning."

She was quiet for a bit, studying the dregs in her glass. "Can I at least ask how?" she said.

"How Matthew died?"

Sarah nodded.

"You don't want to know."

"What does that mean?"

"We were swimming in Lake Michigan and he drowned."

"You were there?"

"Me and my stepfather. Matthew got caught in a riptide. They found his body three days later." I watched her face pale as she realized what I was telling her. "That's right, Sarah. Jake and I both had brothers who drowned when we were kids."

"What does it mean?"

"Probably nothing."

"It doesn't freak you out?"

"I told you the other day, the Wingate letter bothers me. As far as my brother's death goes, there's no connection to Havens."

"You don't know that. What if the person who sent the letter knows about your past and is manipulating you as well?"

"How? I decided to take Z's seminar myself. I didn't tell anyone. No one influenced me. And I didn't receive the Wingate letter. Havens did."

"It's still a little strange if you ask me." Sarah's phone buzzed. She checked the number. "It's Jake." She clicked on her phone. "Hey, we were just talking about you. Yeah, he's right here." Sarah reached over and squeezed my hand. "You want to come over?"

She pulled the phone from her ear. "He's at Medill now." She put the phone back to her ear. "Jake, we're at a place called Clarence's on Central. We've got a table outside." A pause. "Cool. See you then."

Sarah clicked off and slipped her phone onto the table. "He's gonna come over."

"Fine."

"I think you need to tell him about Matthew."

"There's no connection, Sarah."

"We don't know that. We can't know that."

When I didn't respond, she ordered us two more beers. With their arrival the dark talk vanished. At least for the moment. We were sitting and sipping when Havens walked in.

"You guys look like you're having fun. What's up, Joyce?"

I gave him a nod. Sarah patted the seat beside her. Our waitress materialized at Havens's elbow. He ordered whatever we were having and sat back in his chair. "You go to the parade?"

"It was great," Sarah said.

"Why were you at Medill?" I said.

"I was at Wingate's school this morning. A couple more old-timers agreed to meet with me."

"About what?"

Our waitress arrived with Havens's pint. He took a sip. "Good beer. What is it?"

"Daisy Cutter," I said. "Local brew. What did you get at the school?"

He studied me over the rim of his glass. "You need to chill, Joyce."

"Sage advice coming from Mr. Intensity himself. I'm fine, Havens. Now, what did you find at the school?"

"Not much. They all remembered Wingate, of course. No one seemed to have any idea why it happened. I told them about the letter I got."

"You shouldn't have done that."

"Well, I did." Another sip of beer and a smug smile.

"Ian and I were just talking about the letter," Sarah said.

"We were?" I said.

"Sort of." She widened her eyes at me as if to ask permission.

"Go ahead."

So she told Havens about my brother. And how he died. She didn't go into all the details. Just a few, spare facts. Then she tried to tie it into what happened to Havens's brother. When she'd finished, Sarah waited, but Havens demurred.

"Maybe we leave it for another day."

I tipped my pint, the tiniest nudge his way. Sarah sensed the shift and acceded to it, spinning out a new thread of conversation. About the parade. The weather. Evanston. Medill.

We drank for another hour. Sarah cozied her chair up to Jake's, dropping one elbow on the table and tucking a hand under her chin. The closer she got, the less he seemed to speak. I was like a discarded piece to a puzzle no one ever finished anyway. At least that's how I felt. Sarah excused herself to go to the bathroom. And then it was me and Jake.

"You think Sarah's got a point?" he said. "About someone targeting the two of us?"

"Because of our brothers?" I shook my head. "No. They might have picked you out and sent the letter. Figured you'd take it personally once you knew the facts. But they didn't reach out to me."

"Maybe. Anyway, I'm sorry about Matthew."

"Me, too."

We touched glasses. In a splintered moment, we knew more about each other than we could in a million lifetimes. And none of it was happy.

"I was going to head into the city," he said. "Got a friend who has a boat. He goes up and down the lake, checking out the different firework shows. Ten, fifteen people. Beers, some food."

"Thanks, but I think I'm gonna stick close to home tonight."

"You sure?"

"Yeah. I bet Sarah's game."

"I'll ask her."

They insisted on another round of drinks. I said no. Sarah all but dragged me out of my chair, demanding I go with them. To the boat. And Havens's party. Again, I said no. She kissed me when they left. Told me she loved me the way you do when you've had too much to drink and that she'd call. Havens told me he'd pick me up tomorrow afternoon for our meeting with Moncata. Then they were gone. And I was alone. I wandered into the bar and ordered a fresh beer. The Cubs were on, in and of itself enough to make me call it a night. I was toying with that idea, along with a couple of others, when a hand plucked at my shoulder.

"Northwestern?"

I turned to find the young woman from the Street Ministry, dark hair with streaks of gold, smiling and sliding onto the stool next to me. She held out her hand.

"Remember me? Theresa."

27

I took her just inside the door to my house. In the living room, on the coffee table. The next time I remember was in my bed, her hands running across my back, thighs gripping and squeezing. The last time she was above me, eyes closed in concentration, teeth shining, hips moving to their own sweet rhythm. If there was any more after that, it was news to me. I just hoped I had fun.

I woke up at a little after three a.m. Her scent was still on my sheets, but the girl was gone. I felt my way downstairs, the pounding footsteps of a headache close behind. Articles of my clothing were scattered around the living room. Nothing of hers. I sat on the couch and vaguely remembered a second bar after Clarence's. There was a barber's chair, me in it, head back, mouth open. Theresa stood over me with a bottle of tequila and some lime juice. Upside-down margaritas they called them. I licked at the lint in my mouth. Then I got myself a glass of water and five aspirin. I made sure the front door was locked and crawled upstairs. Before I went to sleep, I checked my phone. No messages. I wondered where my two classmates were and fell into the black again.

28

The Street Ministry burned down barely two hours later. Grace Washington hit my cell phone at a little after eight a.m. I was foggy on the details, but she said I needed to come down. Right now. Something in Grace's voice told me I ignored her at my peril, so I dragged myself out of bed and got dressed. The aspirin and water must have helped because I didn't feel half as bad as I deserved.

They had the street roped off with cops redirecting traffic. I found a parking space a couple of blocks away and began to walk. The implications of the fire started to sink in. As did Grace's cryptic warning. And then I thought about Theresa. I wondered if she'd be there. That was when the headache returned in earnest.

Grace was standing in a pile of debris that used to be her office. Now there was nothing left. No roof, no walls. No building. Just a twist of melted plastic and scorched timber. I waited while she finished talking to one of the firefighters. No one else from the ministry seemed to be around. Specifically, no Theresa. I breathed a small sigh of thanks.

"What do you think?" Grace kicked at a pile of plaster as she spoke. There was a simmering anger in her voice, but I wasn't sure where it was focused.

"How did it happen?" I said.

"How do you think? Someone torched it."

"Are they sure?"

"Follow me."

We stepped through the remnants of a wall and into an alley that ran behind the ministry. She walked down about twenty feet and pointed. A couple of firefighters were crouched over a smoking hunk of rubble.

"That used to be our back door. They say it was kicked in. They found gasoline poured along the walls and floors."

"Was anyone inside?"

Grace laughed. "That's the thing. Someone called an hour ahead of time. Told us they were going to burn it so we could clear everyone out."

"What?"

"It was the police, Ian. Worse than any gang. They want to burn, they burn."

"Did you see anybody?"

"Who wants to see? Then what? Snitch on a Chicago cop?"

A fireman dragged a length of hose down the alley and yelled at us to move back.

"They can't," I said.

"They can and they do. You think the neighborhood's gonna care? Hell, they'll throw a party."

Spray from the hose kicked back on us as the fireman began to water down the rubble. We walked inside. Or what was left of it. Grace lit up a cigarette. I didn't think the firemen would appreciate that, but no one was around to stop her.

"I'm sorry," I said.

"Thanks."

"Will you have the money to rebuild?"

She gave me a tight smile. "That's the flip side to dealing with the Chicago PD."

"What does that mean?"

"We keep our mouth shut, let them burn us out, and maybe, maybe, they help with the insurance. Write it up so we get twice as much as the building's worth."

I shook my head.

"Uh-huh." Grace pointed the lit end of her cigarette at me. "Now, you're learning."

"Why did you call me down here?" I said.

"Why do you think?" She took a final drag and dropped the butt to the ground. Smoke streamed out both nostrils as she spoke. "You're the only fresh face that's been in here for a year and a half. Got to be you."

I didn't want to believe it, but I did.

"That's not all," Grace said. "You know the young girl at the desk the day you came in?"

I felt the blood rush to my face and pound in my ears. When I spoke, my voice seemed far away. "The girl?"

"Theresa. Small, Latina, dark."

"Yeah, I remember her."

Grace looked at me out of the corner of her eye. I don't think she liked what she saw. I couldn't blame her.

"She was on the phone. Day before yesterday. Mentioned your name to someone."

"Me?"

"None other. Heard it myself."

"Who was she talking to?"

"Don't know. But she's worked with the police before."

"Worked with them?"

"Theresa's a user. In and out of rehab. Been known to snitch off to the cops to save her skin. I let her work here, but I think that was a mistake."

"She mentioned my name?"

"Yep. I checked the number after she got off, but it was restricted."

"Who do you think it was?"

Grace shrugged like I should know better.

"And you think the cops burned this place down because of me? Because I came by asking about James Harrison?"

"One of the firemen told me whoever did it took special care with this office and our files. Made sure everything burned to a cinder."

"But you gave me nothing, Grace. The inventory report on the jeans, but what the hell is that?"

"They don't know what I had. And they don't know what I gave you. But there's something out there they're worried about. Have you gone to see Sam Moncata?"

I shook my head.

"Go see Moncata. He's a smart man. And the cops aren't likely to mess with him. Better yet, give this whole thing up altogether. The people who did this will hurt you if they have to."

"I'm fine," I said.

Grace snorted. "And stay away from Theresa. Girl's nothing but trouble. You hear me?"

I heard her. In my ear, all the way back to my car. That's when my cell phone buzzed. I half expected it to be Theresa, dropping the other shoe. Instead, it was the father of a dead girl, wanting me to buy him lunch.

29

I met Ned Rolland at a Popeyes on California, just a block from the Criminal Courts Building.

"They only give us a half hour," he said and moved his eyes toward the line at the counter.

"Maybe we should order?" I said.

"Good idea."

He got the six-piece fried chicken dinner with sides of Cajun rice and mac and cheese. I ordered a large Coke.

"You ain't gonna eat?" Ned looked like he didn't trust anyone who didn't eat, so I got a two-piece dinner. We took our food to a booth by the front window. He dug in. I picked at my food and watched.

"What do you do at the courthouse?" I said.

Ned stripped a chicken leg naked and dropped the greasy bone onto a small but growing pile. "I clean the bathrooms." He took a sip from his soft drink. "You been down to the courthouse?"

"Not yet."

"Uh-huh." Ned laid waste to a second leg of chicken and opened up the container of rice. "You smell like smoke."

I smiled. "Been a long morning."

"You said something in your message about my daughter, Rosina."

Rosina Rolland was the name I'd copied off the tombstone Z had visited in Calvary Cemetery. Ned was Rosina's father. I'd done some research online and called him after I left Calvary. "Playing a hunch" is what journalists in the movies called it. Felt like fishing without a pole to me.

"I'm a student at Northwestern's journalism school," I said. "I've got this class where we reopen old murders and try to find out who really did them."

"Rosina wasn't murdered. She died in a car accident."

"Your daughter's buried in Calvary Cemetery in Evanston."

"You don't think I know where she's buried?"

"Yes, sir. I was just wondering, why all the way up in Evanston? I mean, she grew up on the South Side, right?"

Ned halted a forkful of rice halfway to his mouth. "Excuse me?"

"I was wondering, sir . . . and I know it's none of my business . . . but who paid for Rosina's burial expenses?"

"That's what you want to know? Who paid to bury my daughter?"

"Yes, sir."

Ned put down his fork. "Why?"

It wasn't going particularly well, but I didn't see any choice at this point, so I barged ahead. "I think you're wrong, sir. I think your daughter might have been murdered. Or at least it wasn't an accident."

I could see the spark in his eye, the almost involuntary nod of the head. Ned Rolland's only daughter had been dead a long time, but he was still a dad. Which meant I had half a chance.

"I don't know who paid for the burial," he said.

"But someone did?"

"Yes. They insisted Rosina be buried up in Evanston. The whole thing cost some money, so I thought . . ."

"You did what was best for your daughter. Would anyone else know who paid for the arrangements?"

"Someone from the police called and said it was taken care of. That's all I know."

"You don't remember a name?"

"It was twenty years ago."

"How about the funeral home?"

"Funeral home was on the South Side. Burned down a long time now. Why you so interested?"

I shook my head. "If you can't give me a name, it doesn't matter."

"That's it?"

"That's it."

Ned Rolland wiped his mouth and hands with a napkin and packed up the trash from his lunch. Then he got up to leave. I stayed where I was.

"You coming?" he said.

"I'm just gonna sit for a minute if that's all right."

I felt his weight slide back into the booth. "Hey."

I looked up.

"You studying to be a journalist?"

"That's the idea."

"And you think you're gonna get anywhere giving up that quick?"

"I'm not giving up. It's just . . ."

"You said my daughter was murdered. I'm not saying you're right. I'm not saying you're wrong. But there's a few things that always bothered me."

"I'm listening."

"*Now* you listening." Ned shook his head. "You got an hour?"

I checked my watch. Havens was supposed to pick me up at three for our appointment with Moncata. "Sure."

"Good. I've got something at home you might be interested in."

"What about work?"

"Thirty years scrubbing toilets, I'm entitled to an afternoon. Finish your chicken and let's go."

30

By the time I got home, it was just past three. Havens's car was parked in front of my house. I slipped into the front seat.

"Where you been?" he said.

I was tempted to tell him about my lunch with Ned Rolland but decided to keep it to myself for now. Besides, it wasn't like I didn't have plenty of other news. "Street Ministry burned down last night."

Havens whistled. "I'm thinking we got 'em on the run."

"Yeah. Now if we only knew why."

Havens chuckled and slipped his car into gear. "Moncata?"

I pointed to the empty road stretching out ahead of us. "Moncata."

We found Sam Moncata in a midrise not far from Northwestern Hospital. He met us in the lobby and walked us through security. One of the guards asked us to sign in, but the scientist waved her off and pushed us through. We took an elevator to the seventh floor and walked down a long, drab corridor. Moncata stopped before a door that read ITB LABS and swiped his ID through a reader. The door clicked and we were inside.

There was no receptionist. No waiting area. Just two more guards sitting behind a desk. They were watching three security monitors and wearing guns. Moncata led us past what looked like several empty labs to a suite of offices. Moncata's was a good-sized affair, with no windows, a wall of books, and a desk covered with pictures of what looked like grandkids. The man himself was small with a high forehead, bright eyes, and compact features. He looked to be in his mid-sixties and, from all appearances, still humming along at top speed.

"You guys said you were students?" Moncata took a seat behind his desk and gestured for us both to sit. I felt like we were talking to our dad. Or maybe on a job interview.

"Yes, sir," I said. "We're in the innocence seminar at Medill. Professor Zombrowski's seminar."

Moncata nodded vigorously. "Yup, yup. Worked with Judy. Sorry I can't give you a lot of time, but we're in the middle of a couple of things."

"You still working for the police?" Havens said.

"Used to. Chicago PD, then the FBI. But I went private long ago. We're a small outfit, highly specialized. The county hires us when they can afford it. Now, how can I help you?"

"We're working on the James Harrison case," I said.

"Yes, you told me as much over the phone."

"I'm not sure if you remember Grace Washington over at the Street Ministry?"

"You mentioned Grace on the phone as well."

"She says you did the forensic work for Mr. Harrison. On his appeal."

Moncata nodded along with me as I spoke. "Sure did. DNA testing on a bloodstain. I pulled the lab work for you." He pushed forward a black binder.

"Sounds like something about the case might have bothered you?" Havens said.

Moncata shifted in his chair so he could get a better look at my classmate. "And why do you say that, young fella?"

"Busy guy. Couple of students call about an old file, and yet you have time for us."

Moncata obliged us with a smile. "Either of you want something to drink?"

We shook our heads. Moncata got himself a Diet Dr Pepper from a small refrigerator. "You're right." Moncata popped open his drink and poured it into a cup. "Harrison bothers me. Always has."

"Why?" I said.

Moncata slipped on a pair of reading glasses and thumbed through the binder until he found the report he wanted. "We got a thirteen loci match. No doubt about it. The blood they sent us belonged to the victim." He flipped the binder shut. "I guess the thing that bothered me was that Harrison raised money for the testing himself. I mean, who does that? A guy who's guilty knows how it's gonna come back. Anyway, it always bugged me."

"How did you obtain the sample?" I said. "The one you tested?"

"The clerk's office sent it to us."

"What exactly did they send you?" I said.

"Little swatch of fabric from the defendant's jeans. Tagged as evidence and sealed. I signed for it."

"So you get the evidence, do your test, and return the sample?" I said.

Moncata rocked his head from side to side. "Depends. I mean that's how it's *supposed* to work, but sometimes I use up all the sample. Sometimes I just keep whatever I have left. Depends on the case. Depends on the court."

"How about in this case?" Havens said.

"Harrison? Hell, by the time I finished my testing, the man was dead."

"So you never shared your results with the court?" Havens said.

"I forwarded the results, but no one seemed very interested."

"And what about the swatch?" I said. "Do you still have it?"

Moncata flashed another quick grin. "Thought you might ask that." He pulled up a thick case file from the floor and dug through it. "Here she is."

The swatch was a ragged piece of washed-out fabric, maybe an inch square, covered in pencil marks and sealed up in a plastic bag.

"As you can see, pieces have been cut out," Moncata said.

"Can I touch it?" I said.

"Just don't take it out of the bag."

I picked up the Baggie and stared at the tiny piece of cloth, wondering what the hell I'd hoped was going to happen. Then I handed it to Havens, who seemed equally at sea.

"No easy answers, huh?" Moncata returned the swatch to the file and folded his hands over it. He glanced expectantly, first at me, then at Havens. We had nothing. The scientist didn't seem surprised. "Maybe you should just tell me what this is all about."

"We think Harrison might have been framed," I said.

"I figured that much. Why?"

I explained about the ministry's inventory log. And Grace's recollection of the surgical scrubs Harrison was wearing on the night he was arrested. Moncata rubbed his lower lip with his thumb while I talked. When I'd finished, he flipped open the document binder again. This time he took out a one-page report from the Chicago PD. At the top were the words CHAIN OF CUSTODY LOG in large block letters.

"This came with the swatch. It establishes chain of custody. In this case, it indicates the defendant was wearing jeans on the night he was arrested. And the sample we have came from those jeans."

"Not according to Grace," I said.

"Unfortunately, the world doesn't spin according to Grace."

"You said yourself the case bothered you," Havens said.

"Lots of cases bother me, but that doesn't really matter."

"Why not?" I said.

"Because science is science. And when it's the science of DNA, there's not a lot of wiggle room."

"What if someone took the blood from Skylar Wingate's body after he was dead," I said. "Sprinkled it on the jeans."

"What if they did? Blood's blood. Whether the person is alive or dead, I have no real way of knowing."

"So there's no way to tell if this stuff was planted?"

Moncata twitched his lips at the last word and scratched an ear. Just then his phone rang. He looked at the caller ID, then back at us. "You guys mind waiting outside? I've got to take this."

We sat in an empty hallway. A man and a woman in lab coats walked by. Then another man with a gun on his belt. No one gave us a second look.

"What do you think about Moncata?" Havens said.

"Seems like a good guy."

"Should we tell him about the Street Ministry burning down?"

"Hell, no."

We were quiet for a bit more.

"I'm gonna tell him about the other old cases," Havens said. "Scranton and Allen."

"Why?"

"I think they're all connected."

"What if they are? There's nothing he can do. Let's stick to the jeans."

Things got quiet again. This time I broke the silence.

"How was the boat?"

A shrug. "Good time. You should have come."

I tried to catch his eyes, but Havens kept them glued to the floor.

"You guys out late?" I said.

Just then the door opened. Moncata swept us back in with a hand.

"Sorry. Like I said, busy day." He didn't offer us a seat this time. The man was in wrap-up mode and didn't try to hide it. "I'm gonna have to hustle you guys out of here, but let's do this. I'll take a look at the material we have from Harrison. Run a few tests. See if anything interesting shakes out. No promises. In fact, I'm pretty sure we'll turn up nothing. But I won't charge the school for the work and maybe you'll learn something. Fair enough?"

I reached out and shook his hand. "Thanks so much, Mr. Moncata."

"Sam."

I took a card from a holder on his desk. "If it's okay, I'll e-mail you our contact info. We'll follow up next week?"

"Great." Moncata started herding us toward the door. Havens, however, wasn't budging.

"Actually, Sam, I've got one more question."

Moncata checked his watch.

"It won't take a second," Havens said.

Moncata shook his head. "Not a great time, son."

Havens ignored him. "We think there might be two other old cases that are linked to Harrison."

"Write it up and send it to me," Moncata said, now literally pushing us, albeit gently, out of his life.

"They're linked by time, manner of death, proximity to water."

Moncata's phone started ringing again. He looked to me for help.

"Jake, let's go," I said. "We can send him details on the other cases later . . ."

"And they all feature bite marks," Havens said.

Moncata's hand fell off my shoulder. The scientist cocked his head and studied my classmate. "Did you say bite marks?"

"I did."

The phone was still ringing. Moncata ignored it. "Sit down for a second."

So we sat. And Moncata listened as Havens outlined his theory on Billy Scranton and Richmond Allen. Then he showed Moncata paperwork from each case, including the bite-mark photos.

"We believe there was biting on Skylar Wingate as well," Havens said, "but we don't have any photos."

Moncata looked through the material Havens had given him and studied the bite marks with a magnifying glass. Then he put the photos up on a light board and studied them some more.

"Do you have these on a disk?" he said.

"This is all we have," Havens said.

"Do you mind if I keep them for a while? I can assure you they'll be safe."

"We've had problems," Havens said.

Moncata no longer seemed in a hurry. "What sort of problems?"

So we told him. About my traffic stop. And the Street Ministry. And finally, the fire. I left out any mention of Theresa. Right now, I didn't want to think about her myself. When we finished, Moncata was silent. He got up from his chair and began to pace.

"If there was biting in the Harrison case," he said, "it was never brought up at trial."

"We saw a mention of it in Wingate's autopsy report," I said.

Moncata stopped pacing. "Do you have the report?"

"No. The cops took it at the traffic stop."

"Right. Still, there might be a way to get photos of Wingate's body. Let me work on that. If I can get them, I'll send all three cases to a colleague who's an expert in the area. He has a program that can enhance the marks and perhaps tell us a little more."

I'd heard about bite-mark technology, but that didn't explain Moncata's sudden interest. Before I could ask about the change of heart, the scientist again shifted gears.

"You guys ever heard of the Needle Squad?"

We hadn't.

"Downtown everyone just called them the Squad. They were an elite prosecutorial team. About twenty men and women who made their bones in the late eighties and nineties. Renowned for their high conviction rate, especially in capital cases. The leader was a prosecutor named Teddy Green. You've heard of him?"

"He was the Illinois attorney general," Havens said. "Before that he was the state's attorney for Cook County. Dropped dead last year from a stroke."

"He was also lead prosecutor in the Wingate murder," I said.

Moncata shot me with his index finger. "Bingo. Teddy's right-hand man was a Chicago detective named John Carlton." The scientist circled back behind his desk and picked up a couple of the documents we'd given him from the Scranton and Allen murders. Teddy Green's name was on one. John Carlton's on the other. "Looks like they handled your other cases as well."

"What are you saying?" Havens said.

Moncata dropped the documents back onto his desk. "What am I saying? It's a pattern. In forensic science, we like patterns. You should, too. The fact is that Detective Carlton never met a suspect he didn't want to beat a confession out of. And Teddy Green liked to win. Period. So they put together a team and started banging out murder convictions. Indigent defendants. Public defenders. One-day trials. Eventually, Teddy got himself elected attorney general. Carlton became chief of detectives. And everyone lived happily ever after. Except the guys they put in jail. What did they wind up getting your defendant on in the Scranton case?"

"They linked Michael Laramore to the victim through hair and fiber samples," Havens said.

"And how about in the Allen case?"

"Blood typing."

Moncata snorted. "Pure garbage. I assume the bite marks were never mentioned at either trial?"

Havens shook his head.

"Problem is everything was so long ago," Moncata said, talking mostly to himself now. "Green's dead. Carlton, I'm not sure . . ." He typed a few lines into his computer and nodded slowly. "John Carlton. Took retirement in 2005. Died last year."

"There's gotta be something," Havens said.

Moncata tapped a thumbnail against his teeth and stared at the bite-mark photos still up on the light board. "Leave this stuff with me. I'll have my guy take a look at the marks. See what we see. Now I really gotta run." Moncata got up from behind his desk and showed us to the door. "I'll call you if I find anything."

31

Jake and I didn't talk much on the ride back to Evanston. Moncata had thrown out a lot of new pieces, and I think we were both trying to absorb them all. Havens pulled his car up in front of my house.

"Well?" he said.

"Moncata certainly perked up when you mentioned the bite marks."

"Sure did."

"Do you still trust him?"

"Not entirely. You?"

"I don't know. What about Z?"

"What about her? She's gotta stay in the dark. At least until we know if our three cases are connected."

"Moncata knew more than he told us," I said.

Havens's phone buzzed with a text. He checked it and turned the phone off.

"What is it?" I said.

Havens killed the engine. "I've been doing a little digging on how James Harrison died in prison."

"Yeah?"

"This morning I talked to a retired Stateville guard named Vince Shumpert. He told me the guy who ran the guards inside the Department of Corrections set up Harrison. A guy named Brian Hines."

"What do you mean 'set up'?"

"Shumpert said the rumor was Hines paid a gang to kill Harrison inside Menard prison. Then I asked about the other two. Laramore and Tyson."

"The ones who were convicted on Scranton and Allen?"

"Word is Hines wired those two as well."

"Wow."

"Here's the kicker. The detective Moncata mentioned today as part of the Needle Squad, John Carlton?"

"What about him?"

"Shumpert just texted me that Carlton was Brian Hines's cousin."

"Where's Hines now?"

"Dead from a stroke."

"Is it my imagination," I said, "or are a lot of people having strokes?"

An Evanston police car cruised past, silent flashers rolling. We watched until it disappeared down the street.

"You think we're safe up here?" Havens said. "In Evanston, I mean?"

"Don't count on it." I hadn't told my classmates about the break-in at my house. Or the cop's hat band I'd found on my mom's bed. It's something I'd wonder about later.

"I guess we should call Sarah," Havens said. "Catch her up."

The subject had lain fallow, pushed to the back burner by our meeting with Moncata and all the rest. Now there was a shadow in Havens's voice at the mention of her name, and I knew they'd been together.

"Why don't you give her a call," I said. "I'm going to review everything we have. Try to organize things a bit."

"Okay." He seemed suddenly anxious to get away. I thought that might be a good idea all around.

"Let's talk tomorrow," I said.

"Be careful, Joyce."

"You, too."

I climbed out of the car. Havens pulled away from the curb and was gone. I walked into the house and made a pot of coffee. While it brewed, I thought about Jake and Sarah. Not good. I needed to keep myself busy, my mind occupied. I went into the living room with my coffee and a fresh pad of paper. I wrote down everything I could remember from the visit with Moncata. Then I took out the material Ned Rolland had given me and put it in a separate file marked *Rosina Rolland—Accident.* After that I reviewed all the evidence we'd collected, sifting, condensing, and refining until I had it cooked down to seven pages on a legal pad. I pulled an old bulletin board out of a closet, found some thumbtacks and a set of index cards. On the first card I wrote: *Scranton—Wingate—Allen* and thumbtacked it to the board. Then I filled out a half-dozen or so more cards and began putting them up. When I'd finished, the board looked something like this:

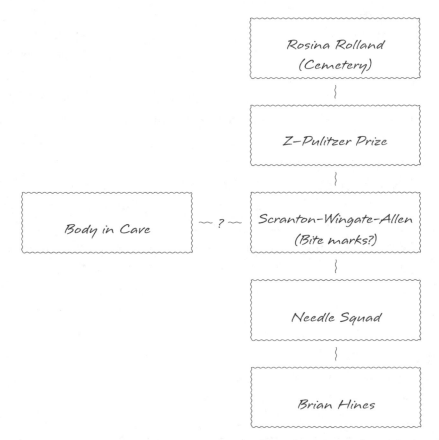

I was playing around with the cards, taking some off and rearranging what was left when I felt a breeze. I'd left the front door ajar and got up to close it. Z stood in the doorway. I should have been surprised, but I wasn't.

"Hi."

"Forgive me for barging in," she said.

"It's fine. Come on in." I walked her into the living room and turned up the lights. My research lay all over the floor. I began to clean up, pulling the index cards off the bulletin board and sticking them in my pocket.

"For the seminar?" she said.

"Yeah. We've been working on a few things. You want to sit down?"

I cleared some space on the couch. Z took a seat.

"I'm not really ready to go over any of this," I said, doing my best to push files out of sight.

"Not a problem."

I took a spot beside her on the couch. Up close I could see a cloud of red veins running through both cheeks. Her lips were wet and there was a glint of something desperate in her eyes.

"I need to ask you a question, Ian."

"Sure."

"Why did you take my seminar?"

I shrugged. "I'm interested in the subject matter and was lucky enough to get a spot."

"How interested?"

"I'm not following you."

"Perhaps a better way to put it is why are you interested?"

"The criminal justice system fascinates me. This is an opportunity to get involved. Rather than just reading about it."

"And your goal with all this"—Z gestured to the debris around us— "is to right a wrong? Find a case where a man's been wrongfully convicted and prove his innocence?"

"Of course. Why all the questions?"

"I've been teaching the seminar for more than a decade now. Never had an inquiry from the police until Detective Rodriguez called the other day. That bothers me."

"I understand."

"I'm not sure you do. Rodriguez is convinced you have an agenda. Some other reason for being in my class. I'd like to know what that might be."

"I don't have an agenda, ma'am. Perhaps we, or I, made a mistake going to the forest preserve. But we were eager to get going. Make something happen, I guess. We had no idea there was a body there."

"Whose idea was it to go into the woods?"

"We decided together. Over a few beers. I know, stupid."

"Stupid's one word for it."

"We've apologized," I said. "I'm not sure what else I can do."

Z allowed the silence to build. I imagined she'd used the tactic many times in her career as a journalist. Probably to pretty good effect.

"How well do you know your classmates?" she finally said. "Ms. Gold, for example?"

"We graduated together. But I wouldn't say I know her well."

Z sharpened her eyes a touch. I wasn't sure if I was lying, but it definitely felt like it.

"And Mr. Havens?"

"Never met him until last week."

"You three getting along?"

"Can I ask why you're so interested?"

"Certainly. It's a small class. One of the first things I have to do is take the temperature. See who fits together and who doesn't."

"We get along just fine."

"There are always differences between students. Backgrounds, personalities. Some are more . . ." She paused, eyes searching my living room ceiling for the right word. "More fragile than others."

"We're all pretty tough."

Z studied me. There was a hard cast to her mouth that softened as quickly as it appeared. "That's good to hear, Ian." She picked up one of my files without looking at it. "Have you made any progress on Harrison?"

I took the file out of her hand. "I think we'll have something for you."

"By next week?"

"I hope so."

"Wonderful. Well, I guess I'd better get going." We walked to my front hallway, where she checked her reflection in a mirror. For a moment I saw her as a woman and suddenly wondered what she did with her nights. Boyfriend? Bars? Home with a movie and some takeout? I wondered when was the last time she'd gotten herself laid. Maybe she was reading my mind. Or maybe I was reading hers.

"I'm going into the city tonight," she said. "A play at the Goodman."

I didn't respond.

"Don't worry, Ian, I'm not asking you to go with me. It's not like I even have an extra ticket." Her laugh was loud and harsh. Like the bray of a donkey, except bordering on hysterical.

"I wasn't thinking that, ma'am."

She waved a long, thin hand. "Never mind. What are your plans for tonight?"

"I've got a few more things here I need to do."

"I just saw your classmates downtown. At that Irish pub. What is it? Nevin's?"

"Yeah."

"Mr. Havens and Ms. Gold. Looked like they were having a nice time. Are you planning on joining them?" Another small, hard smile.

"In fact, I probably will."

"Glad to hear it. Thanks for taking the time to chat. If you need any help, feel free to give me a call. That's what I'm here for."

I shut the door behind her and took a look at myself in the mirror. Fucking bitch. Twenty minutes later, I locked up my house and headed out for the night.

32

They got to her place at a little after one in the morning. I could tell by the mincing steps she took and the way he held her elbow that she was drunk. They stopped on the front porch. She lifted her head and her shoulders shook with laughter. She almost lost her balance and reached out to grab his shirt. An arm slipped around her waist. I moved my eyes to the rearview mirror. A smear of headlights approached. A dark sedan swept past and kept going. Then a second. I turned up the radio and looked back at the porch. They had their backs to me, and Sarah was finding a key to unlock the front door. Jake turned and stared right at me, but I knew he couldn't see anything. The door popped open. He held it and they both went in. It was three flights up to her apartment, a full minute before a light came on. Then, a second. I watched their silhouettes float back and forth across the room. A hand pulled the curtains shut. Ten minutes after that, the lights went out.

The radio was tuned to an all-news station. They freshened the headlines every six minutes. I listened to three updates and then got out. Havens's Honda was parked under a streetlight. I looked inside and saw a shovel in the back and a green tarp. I went back to my car. Six updates later, a light in the living room came back on. A hand tugged the curtains open. Twelve minutes after that, Havens appeared on the front porch, alone. I waited until he'd left. Then I waited ten more minutes. I got out of the car, locked it, and walked toward Sarah Gold's apartment.

33

The young boy stared at the four-letter word glowing on the screen of his phone. HOME. He tapped the screen and the phone number itself appeared. The 410 area code sent a jumble of feelings through him. Sadness. Warmth. Pity. Fear. He thought he'd be used to being alone by now. But he just couldn't toughen up. A door kicked open at the far end of the alley. He slipped the phone into his pocket and doused his cigarette.

"Luke? Where the fuck are you? We got a full house in there. God-damnit, Luke?"

The door slammed shut and Luke was alone again. He worked as a bar-back at a place called Timbers in Chicago's Boystown. He'd only gotten the job because they thought he was gay and might bring in customers. Luke let them think what they wanted. It wasn't the first time he'd used his looks to gain an edge. Then his fat-fuck pig of a boss had come on to him. Luke should have expected it. Still, it disgusted him. But he needed the money. So he gave the pig some halfway decent head. Not the first time he'd gained an edge that way either.

Luke stared at his name, tattooed in thin lines of ink across the inside of his wrist. Stupid thing he'd done messing around with his buddies back home. When they were all gonna head out to California together. He felt the thick pad of cash in his pocket and smiled to himself. The bar's safe was in the basement. The pig kept the combination in his wallet. Easy pickings. Luke hadn't counted it all. Just took whatever was there. Maybe five hundred. Enough, at least, for a ticket back to Maryland. He took the phone out of his pocket and pulled up his mom's number again. Then he hit SEND. The number rang once. Luke disconnected and stared at the screen.

"You gonna call her, or not?"

Luke nearly pissed himself. The man who'd spoken shifted into the light and chuckled. He was old, with narrow yellow eyes and long, curved features. His hair was shiny and slicked back from his forehead in smooth strokes.

"What's her name?" the man said.

"Who?"

"The girl you're thinking of calling."

"It wasn't a girl."

"Home, then."

Luke slipped the phone back into his pocket.

"How old are you?"

"Thirteen."

"Where you from?"

"Baltimore."

The man nodded like Baltimore was just what he expected. "I came back here for a smoke." He looked expectantly at Luke, who pulled out a pack of cigarettes. They both lit up. Luke streamed blue smoke into the night and leaned against the wall. The alley was long and twisting, but he couldn't stay too long. Not with Timbers's weekly float in his back pocket.

"You're a bar-back at Timbers?" the man said.

"And you're a customer?"

"I come in sometimes for the special. PBR longnecks for a buck and a half."

"Tuesday and Thursday nights. Can't beat it."

"I'm not a fag, Luke."

"I don't care, mister. And how did you know my name?"

"I heard your boss. Seems like he might be looking for you." The man tossed his cigarette away. He wore a pair of faded jeans and boots with rundown heels.

"I'm done with that place," Luke said.

"Not treating you right, huh?"

"I just need to get out of Chicago."

"Headed home?"

"Maybe."

"You need money for the fare?"

"I got plenty."

"You mean what you took from the bar."

Luke came off the wall. "Fuck you, mister."

The man's nostrils flared. Like a feral cat scenting prey. Luke felt a chill.

"I gotta get going," he said.

The man took out a roll of bills. "Two hundred for a suck."

Luke was tempted. It was all of ten minutes' work. And he could always use money. Still, not the best idea. Not with the pig looking for him.

"Another time, mister."

The man counted out another hundred and put it with the rest on the ground between them. He used a rock to hold the money down.

"That's a lot of cash to leave lying around, mister."

"Three hundred. Till I'm dry."

Luke caught the yellow gleam again in the man's eyes and took it to be lust. "Fine, let's go." He scooped up the cash, and they walked together into the deepest part of the alley. The man leaned up against a wall. Luke reached for his crotch.

"Let's see what you got."

The man undid his belt. Luke dropped to his knees. He never saw the rock the man carried in his left hand. Never felt the blow that cracked his skull sideways off the wall. The man with the yellow eyes dragged him another twenty yards, to a van with blacked-out windows, parked in a lot reserved for customers of Cathy's Cupcakes. He lifted the boy into the back of the van. A phone dropped out of the boy's pants pocket and began to vibrate. The man picked it up. The screen registered an incoming call from HOME. The man shook his head and turned it off. Then he went to work on his latest catch.

34

The sun shone through my bedroom window. I rolled over and tried to ignore the banging inside my head. That's when I realized it wasn't in my head at all. I went into the bathroom and splashed cold water on my face. Then I looked at my reflection in the mirror. Whoever was at the front door wasn't going away. I went back into the bedroom and threw on a pair of jeans. In the top drawer of my dresser were copies of the bite-mark photos from Jake Havens's two cases. I considered them in the morning light. More banging at the front door. I stuffed the photos back under my clothes, took a final look in the bedroom mirror, and hustled downstairs.

There were two of them. The same two who had pulled me over a week earlier. I knew by now they liked to do things that way. Let you know who was the hunter and who was the hunted. The black detective showed me his star. The white guy did the talking.

"Mr. Joyce?"

"Yeah?"

"I'm Detective Marty Coursey."

"I think we met a few days ago," I said.

"This is my partner, Nate Johnson. Can we come in?"

I stepped aside and they were in.

"You live alone, Mr. Joyce?" Johnson had picked up the narrative. Coursey wandered into my living room and began touching things.

"Yes," I said. "What's this about?"

"We wake you up?" Johnson said.

"Matter of fact you did. Why?"

"No reason. Just past noon is all."

"I like to sleep in. Could you ask your partner to come in where I can see him?"

"Is he bothering you, Mr. Joyce?"

"Yes, he is."

"Marty?"

Coursey walked back into the hallway and slid the sunglasses up on his forehead. His eyes were colorless, and I could smell cigarettes on his clothes.

"Maybe we can all sit down?" Johnson said.

We settled in the living room, the two detectives on the couch, me in the recliner.

"We're from Violent Crimes," Johnson said.

I sat up in my chair.

"We're going to need a statement from you," Johnson said. "We'd also like permission to search your home and vehicle."

"No one's searching anything," I said. "And I'm not giving any sort of statement until I know what's going on."

"Where were you last night?" Coursey's teeth were yellow and pointed.

I shook my head.

"I figured as much." Coursey stood, gun creaking on his belt as he moved. "Get up, son."

"Why?"

Coursey had his cuffs out. "Get up."

"Hang on, Marty." Johnson put a hand on his partner's arm.

"Just tell me what this is about?" My indignation had dissolved into uncertainty. My demands into pleas, which was exactly what they wanted. Get me scared. Get me talking.

"It's about a sexual assault," Johnson said. "Your classmate, Sarah Gold. Someone broke into her apartment last night and raped her."

"Sarah?" The word dropped from my mouth like a dry pebble.

"Beat the fuck out of her, too." Coursey was close enough now that he could smell the panic.

"If you could give us an accounting of your whereabouts for last night," Johnson said, "we might be able to clear some things up."

"An accounting of my whereabouts?"

"Yes, Mr. Joyce. Where were you last night?"

"I want a lawyer."

Coursey turned to Johnson with a look that said *I told you so*, then turned back to me. "Stand up and put your hands behind your back."

I did. They cuffed me, threw me in the back of an unmarked car, and took me downtown.

35

They handcuffed me to a chair in an empty booking area and left me there for the better part of the afternoon. When Coursey finally came in, he didn't say a word. Just took me to a cell. There was a white kid named Randall lying in the upper bunk. I sat in the lower. Randall told me he was looking at twenty-five to life for running dope. I didn't respond. Randall swung down off his bunk and stood over me, heavy arms resting on the iron bed frame. I felt my heart pump and my blood heat.

"Get away from me." My voice sounded surprisingly even.

"You gonna bite, little pup?" Randall squatted, studying me like I was some sort of strange food they'd put in his dish. "Look at me, little pup."

I did. His eyes were black sinkholes. Skin, prison pale and scarred with ink. He flexed a biceps. "You like?"

I clenched and unclenched my fists. "Fuck you."

"I might just do that." His laugh was heavy, full of smoke and menace. "You don't think that's funny?"

"I think you better kill me, or I'll gut you like a fish."

The laughter stopped, and Randall pulled out the business end of a shank. "Now that you mention it."

I went at him with both hands, hunting for the eyes. Randall wasn't stupid. Or old. He used my momentum to take me to the floor. Then he was on top of me, a knee in my back. I thought about Jake Havens pinning Sarah's ex to the floor in Nevin's. Seemed like a long time ago.

"What you think now, little pup?"

The shank tickled my cheek, and I could feel his breath in my ear. He'd take my life. And so easily. That was the part that really pissed me off.

I reached back and clawed again at his face. Randall grabbed a hunk of hair and pulled my head back. I waited for the slash across the throat and the blood. Preferred it to anything else my cellmate might have planned. Instead, the pressure eased. Randall climbed back into his berth. I pulled myself off the floor and crawled back into mine. Minutes passed. I closed my eyes and listened to my own strangled breathing until it settled. It was my cellmate who spoke first.

"You're in for rape."

My eyes flicked open.

"Them cops offered me a deal to snitch."

"Why?"

"I was gonna ask you the same thing. What's your name?"

"Ian. Ian Joyce."

"Well, Ian Joyce, the machine got you now. So maybe it don't matter."

"Why did you let me go?"

"That's my business." There was a pause. Then the steel shank dropped from the upper bunk onto mine. Its handle was wrapped in gray tape. "Next time someone gets up in you like I did, stick him. First time. First thing. Maybe you'll be all right."

"I'm not gonna be in here too long."

Randall rolled over and yawned. "Keep the shank. And learn how to use it."

Five minutes later, my cellmate was snoring. The adrenaline rush had left me jittery, and I had no idea what time it was. I only knew there was no way I was going to fall asleep. Right up until I did exactly that.

———

Somewhere a steel door slid open and slammed shut. I opened my eyes and studied the springs on the bottom of Randall's bunk. The shank he'd given me was under my pillow. I felt for it. The footsteps got closer, then stopped. A female officer stood just outside my cell. She had a set of cuffs and a belly chain in her hands.

"Ian Joyce?"

I came up off my bunk. I'd never been so happy to hear my name. "I'm Joyce."

"Back up, please."

I moved back from the bars and wondered how long I'd been out. The officer came in and cuffed me. Randall kept his face turned to the wall. The officer took me to an interrogation room with a tinted mirror running the length of one wall. I sat in a chair and swore to myself, no matter what, I wouldn't go back to the cell. Then the door opened. Coursey came in alone. He was wearing a different suit than the last time I saw him and carrying a soft briefcase with a Chicago police crest on it.

"How you doing, college boy?"

"I'd like a lawyer."

Coursey pulled out a set of keys. "How about I undo those bracelets?" He stepped close and undid my handcuffs, then the belly chain. "Better?"

"Thanks."

"You know where you are?" Coursey wrapped and unwrapped the chain around the meat of his fist as he spoke.

"I'm in a police station."

"You're in the fun house, son." Coursey gestured to the glass behind him. "Two-way mirror, right?"

"I suppose so."

"Ain't no one back there." He clattered the chain down on the table and unzipped the briefcase. From inside it, he pulled out a clear plastic bag.

"I like this. Put it over the fucker's head and watch him turn blue." Coursey held the bag up in front of me. "How long you think it would take before you signed whatever I wanted you to sign? I can tell you . . . not long."

The plastic bag disappeared, replaced by a black folder. "Know what this is?"

I shook my head.

"Believe it or not, it's worse than a fucking bag over your head. This here is evidence. More than enough to punch your ticket to Stateville. I figure you for dead inside a month. And it won't be pretty."

"If you don't have the balls to do it yourself, Detective, just say so."

Coursey was no different than my cellmate. If he wanted to have his fun, he'd have to work for it.

"Where were you last night?"

The question caught me off guard. Maybe that was the point, because I found myself answering.

"I went out for a beer."

"Where?"

"Pete Miller's Steakhouse. It's in Evanston."

Coursey took out a pad of paper and wrote something down. "Who were you with?"

"I was by myself."

The detective looked up, then returned to his questions. "How about after Miller's?"

"I went home."

"What time?"

"Eleven. Eleven-thirty."

Coursey put the pad aside and looked at me. Then he read me my rights. "You understand all that?"

He should have done that before he started to question me, but I got the sense it didn't really matter. In the end, it would happen whatever way Coursey said it happened.

"Am I under arrest?" I said.

"Shut up." Another pause. "You were home by eleven-thirty?"

"Yes."

He was back to taking notes. "Can anyone confirm that?"

"I told you. My house was empty except for me."

Coursey pulled a picture out of the unmarked folder and put it down in front of me. "This was taken from a traffic camera on Sarah Gold's block. You see that?"

I knew what Coursey was pointing to. It was my car, idling under a streetlight.

"We had the plates blown up," Coursey said. "Your car, Joyce. The time stamp is twelve forty-seven a.m." Coursey held up a thick finger. "First lie. Breaks the cherry. You want to keep going?"

"Since when is it illegal to sit in your car on the street?"

Coursey nodded his head. He had me talking now and knew I wouldn't stop. He reached into his folder again. This time it was a close-up of Sarah Gold. Her left eye was half closed. The other stared back at me.

"Banged her around pretty good, Joyce."

I pushed the picture away.

"What were you doing in the car?"

"I want a lawyer."

"We have a witness who saw you on her street. Witness puts it at around two-thirty."

"Your witness is mistaken."

Coursey shook his head and chuckled. He pulled out a third photo and stacked it on top of the first two. "How about this one, college boy?"

It looked like another shot from a traffic camera. My profile, caught in a wash of light. I had my hands jammed in my pockets and was walking toward Sarah Gold's apartment. It was bad, but not nearly enough for a jury. At least that's what I hoped. And then there was Sarah herself. What would she say?

"She didn't see her attacker," Coursey said, seeming to read my mind. "And you're probably thinking none of this is enough."

I felt my face grow hot. Definitely reading my mind.

"If you were a nigger," Coursey said, "or a spic, forget it. You'd be flushed in a heartbeat. But you're not a nigger. And Sarah Gold is whiter than you are. People are gonna care about her. And they're gonna remember you. That's why we're gonna get the rest." Coursey began to pack up his materials.

"The rest of what?" I said.

"Forensics. From what I hear, they pulled a nice load out of her."

The first thing I thought of was Sarah and Jake—a jumble of images that flared and died in the same breath. "Are you saying there's DNA to test?"

"And they say Northwestern's a dummy school."

"I didn't rape her, Detective. And I didn't have consensual sex with her."

"The second part, I believe."

"If there's material to test, then I'll be cleared. Simple as that."

"You just don't get it, do you, college boy?" Coursey walked behind my chair and hooked me up, squeezing the cuffs until they bit. Then he leaned down and whispered in my ear. "If we decide we need someone's DNA somewhere, we figure out a way. Whatever it takes." Coursey picked up his briefcase and headed for the door. "Welcome to the fun house, Joyce. Make yourself at home."

And then he left.

36

I sat in the room and tried to latch onto a productive train of thought. But all I could think about was DNA. If they had it. If they really had it. James Harrison's face flashed before my eyes. And the others. Mug shots and numbers. Case files stacked up. Shelf after shelf. Paper and ink. Now flesh and blood. My flesh. My blood. Fifteen minutes crawled by. Then another fifteen. My hands were numb from the pinch of the cuffs. Maybe that was Coursey's plan. Cut off my circulation and kill me in pieces. Hands, arms, legs. I'd wind up like the Black Knight from *Monty Python*. I thought about that scene and almost laughed. Jesus, I was fucking delirious. Maybe *that* was Coursey's plan. I figured he was watching, so I made my face blank. Just then the doorknob turned. Someone was trying to get back into the room. Asking for a key. Muffled voices. Then the sound of metal scraping inside a lock. The knob turned again, and the door opened. Judy Zombrowksi walked in.

"You make a splash, Mr. Joyce. I'll give you that."

Z took the chair Coursey had been sitting in. Vince Rodriguez followed close behind. The detective walked around and snapped off my cuffs. I rubbed my wrists and looked at my professor.

"What are you doing here?"

"What am I doing here?" Z shook her head.

"Where's Sarah?"

"Never mind about Sarah. You need to focus on you."

Neither of my visitors seemed inclined to say anything further, so I waited.

"You realize why you're here?" Z said.

"I didn't rape Sarah."

"You were seen outside her apartment in the middle of the night."

Z must have spoken with Coursey. I wondered if she was part of his strategy. Maybe she was being used by the cops. Get her to get me talking. But wasn't I already talking? And why was Rodriguez here?

On cue, he spoke. "Ian, we're going to take a ride."

"When?"

"Right now. We'll fill you in as we drive."

They took me out a side entrance. Z on one side. Rodriguez on the other. Coursey was nowhere in sight. We walked through a fenced-in police lot to a silver Crown Vic. It felt like the middle of the night, but I couldn't be sure. Rodriguez directed me to the backseat of the car. Z got in beside me. I very much noticed they didn't cuff me.

Rodriguez pulled out of the parking lot and stopped at a red light. "How are you feeling, Ian?"

"Hungry."

"Good. Let's stop." We drove a handful of blocks in silence. Rodriguez pulled into a hole-in-the-wall Mexican joint called Flaco's Tacos. We got a booth by the window. The waitress brought us menus and left. The way she smiled at Rodriguez told me it wasn't the first time he'd been here.

I took a sip of water. It was warm with a shadow of something floating near the top that might have once been ice. The waitress came back with a bowl of chips and salsa. I ordered chicken tacos with rice and a Coke. Z had an iced tea. Rodriguez got himself a *horchata*.

"Am I still under arrest?" I said and reached for the bowl of chips. I noticed a clock on the wall. There was no guarantee it was working, but it read 3:15.

"You were never under arrest," Z said and glanced at Rodriguez. "At least not that I heard."

The detective shook his head. "No charges filed. No paper trail of anything that happened today."

"What did happen today?" I said.

Z leaned forward. "Let's start with last night."

"Fine."

"Were you at Sarah's apartment?"

"Did you see the pictures?"

Z nodded.

"Then why do you ask?"

Rodriguez stirred his drink and took a sip. "Calm down, Ian."

"I'm fine."

The waitress brought my food. Rodriguez waited until I'd polished off a taco before continuing. "Why were you at Sarah's?"

"That's my business."

"It would be better if you told us."

"Why do I feel like I'm still being questioned?"

"The detective's trying to help you," Z said.

"All of a sudden everyone's trying to help." I wasn't hungry anymore and pushed the plate away. "How is she?"

"She'll recover," Rodriguez said.

"And why are you convinced I didn't attack her?"

"Who says I'm convinced of that?"

"So you think I raped her?"

"We don't," Z said.

"All due respect, you're not the one with the badge."

The restaurant was empty, just us and the waitress. The traffic outside the open door was suddenly loud in the street and a radio played Spanish music somewhere.

"My guess is you were in the wrong place at the wrong time," Rodriguez said. "And you still might be."

"What does that mean?"

Rodriguez threw a few dollars on the table. "Your professor's heading back to Evanston. You're gonna need to lay low until we can get a handle on a few things."

"Lay low?"

"We'll find somewhere safe." Rodriguez climbed to his feet. "Come on. Let's get out of here."

As we left, I looked back through the window. The waitress was sitting in our booth, munching on some chips under the hard light and drinking whatever was left of Rodriguez's *horchata*.

37

"This is somewhere safe?" I said.

We were walking down a short, stained hallway toward a metal door—the business end of the Cook County Morgue.

"There's someone I want you to talk to," Rodriguez said. "And I want to keep it between us."

More games. At this point I didn't care. The morgue was a step up from spending the night in a cell with Randall and his pals. Rodriguez hit a few buttons on a keypad and the door opened into a long gray room that looked like an industrial garage. I expected some sort of smell, but all I got was the faintest taste of chemicals on my tongue and a chill that soaked to the bone. Large overhead fixtures cast blue light on three examining tables. Each was made of stainless steel, with a narrow trough running around all four sides and feeding into a drain. There was a large block on one end of the table, presumably to hold the head of the corpse, and a sink at the other. Two of the tables were empty. The third had a body under a white sheet. Sam Moncata stood off to one side of the room, staring at a picture on a light board. He switched off the board as we came in.

"Vince, how are you?" Moncata shook hands with Rodriguez, then turned to me. "I didn't think we'd see each other so soon."

"Me neither," I said.

Moncata showed us into a small break room, just off the main autopsy area but still within sight of the body. There was a table covered with paperwork, some chairs, a coffeemaker, and a row of vending machines. Moncata gestured for us to sit and looked expectantly at Rodriguez.

"I thought you might walk him through it, Sam."

"Fair enough." Moncata brought his fingertips together and turned his full attention to me. "You're probably wondering why the detective brought you here? In the middle of the night, no less?"

"Among other things."

"The last time we spoke, I told you I was busy with an active case." Moncata pointed at Rodriguez. "It's the detective's investigation. A young boy found in a cave inside the Cook County forest preserve."

"I know a little bit about it," I said.

"The detective told me. Your business card being found near the scene. That's not my concern." Moncata paused for a moment. "We've got another victim on the table out there. Male. Thirteen years old. Pulled out of the water six hours ago. About two miles from the first body." Another pause. Whatever Moncata was getting at, he was finding it difficult. "Maybe we should go back into the examining room for a moment?"

We shuffled into the next room and stopped in front of the autopsy table. I looked down at the covered corpse. The boy's arm peeked out from under the sheet. I could just make out an *L* and a *U* tattooed in green spider scrawl across the inside of his wrist. I thought Moncata was going to pull the sheet and give me the full cook's tour. Instead, he walked over to the light board and turned it on. "Over here, Ian. There's something I want you to see."

I moved closer. Rodriguez was on my shoulder, watching both of us. Moncata had two photos on the board. Tight shots of dead flesh.

"Do you know what you're looking at?" he said.

"I'm guessing some kind of autopsy shots?"

"These are bite marks." Moncata pointed with a pencil to first one photo, then the other. "This one is from the boy we found in the cave. This is from the one on the table. Now, come over here."

Moncata led me to a small workstation and a computer. He clicked on the Cook County logo, then a desktop file. The two bite-mark photos appeared on-screen. Moncata hit a few more keys, and one image lifted, then laid itself over the other. "This is some of the bite-mark software I was telling you about the last time we talked. As you can see, when we sharpen these up and compare them, the bite patterns are nearly identical."

I glanced at Rodriguez, who pushed my attention back to the scientist's presentation.

"You and your friend brought me two more bite marks the other day," Moncata said. "The files were roughly fifteen years old." Moncata pulled up the photos we'd given him, fiddled a bit, and then layered them, one after the other, over the first two. Again, the match was nearly perfect.

"I was also able to get a photo of the bite mark found on Skylar Wingate." Moncata glanced at me for a reaction, then pulled up a final shot and laid it over the first four. "Voilà."

"Are you saying all these marks were made by the same person?" I said.

"That's what the evidence is saying, son."

I turned to Rodriguez, who was continuing to study me.

"What do you think?" he finally said.

"I have no idea."

"What's your first impression?"

"It doesn't seem possible."

"Why?"

"Skylar Wingate was killed fourteen years ago. Where's this guy been?"

Moncata took that as his cue to shut down the computer. We went back into the break room and took our seats again.

"You're right," Rodriguez said. "None of this makes sense. But remember what I told you about facts. We go where they take us. And right now this is where we're at."

"How good is the science?" I said. "I mean, the bite marks?"

Rodriguez raised an eyebrow. "Sam?"

"It's not DNA," Moncata said. "But it's not garbage either. There are some discrepancies, but the overall similarity is very strong in at least four of the five cases. It would be hard to imagine those bites not coming from the same person."

"We can't afford to ignore it," Rodriguez said. "Right now, I have to assume there's at least a fair chance that whoever this guy is, he killed those boys years ago and, for some reason has gone active again."

I shook my head. "Maybe you're right, but I still don't understand why I'm here."

"Sam told me he gave you and Havens some background on the Needle Squad."

"He told us a little bit."

"You think the Squad framed James Harrison? And the other two you've been looking at?"

"We can't prove a thing."

A soft smile touched Rodriguez's lips. "Sam?"

Moncata cleared some space on the table and unrolled a white sheet of paper. It was a graph with different-colored lines and numbers running across the top and bottom.

"After you and your pal left the other day, I had our lab do some testing on the blood swatch from Harrison's jeans," Moncata said. "We ran what we call a gas chromatography–mass spectrometry test. Got some interesting results." Moncata pointed to a green line spiking in several places on the chart. "See this, here and here? It tells us that the blood on the jeans, the victim's blood, was loaded with citric acid."

I stared at the jagged lines and shrugged. "What does that mean?"

"Citric acid doesn't occur naturally in human blood, Ian. At least not in these amounts."

"So how did it get there?"

"Citric acid is a preservative. It's often used to preserve blood samples taken at autopsies."

"Someone took this blood from a test tube," Rodriguez said. "Most likely one of Skylar Wingate's autopsy samples."

"And they planted it on James Harrison's jeans," I said.

"That's what they're worried about," Rodriguez said. "That you might get hold of a swatch. And someone like Sam would be smart enough, and curious enough, to run the right test."

Despite everything else, I couldn't help but enjoy the moment. We'd done something. Actually proved something. When no one believed we could.

"What about the other two cases?" I said. "Scranton and Allen?"

Moncata spread his hands. "Bring me some evidence to test."

I looked at Rodriguez. "There's more to this than just Harrison."

"I agree."

"You do?"

"Let's talk about your arrest today."

I felt a slow, cold rumble in my stomach. "Okay."

"Did the detectives mention any sort of DNA evidence?"

"Detective Coursey did, yeah."

Rodriguez glanced at Moncata, who dug into his files again. "Remember this?" The scientist laid down the chain of custody report from 1998 for Harrison's jeans.

"Sure," I said. The slow rumble had become a hot churn.

"Look at the officer's signature."

Marty Coursey's name was scrawled across the bottom of the page.

"Coursey was one of the rank-and-file uniforms on the Needle Squad," Moncata said. "Laid the groundwork for a lot of scientific testimony that came in. A real prick, as I recall."

"I can vouch for that," I said.

"So it was Coursey who told you they had DNA?" Rodriguez said.

I nodded.

"Did he say it was yours?"

"He seemed pretty sure."

Rodriguez glanced again at Moncata. Neither man seemed surprised.

"I didn't rape Sarah, Detective. I went by the house. I guess I was jealous or something. I don't really know. But I didn't go in. And I didn't rape her." The words came out in a rush. As if once spoken, they'd somehow wipe the slate clean.

"I believe you," Rodriguez said. "Not that it's gonna matter."

"What does that mean?"

Rodriguez pulled out a photo and held it facedown in front of him. "I need you to ID someone, Ian."

"Okay."

He slid the photo across and turned it over. I took one look. Then my late-night taco feast came up all over Sam Moncata's table.

38

They cleaned me up. Then they cleaned up the table. Moncata thought the whole thing was pretty funny. Even bragged to Rodriguez he'd seen it coming. I lay down on a small couch they had tucked against a wall. Sam got me a Sprite out of one of the vending machines. Rodriguez pulled his chair close and told me to sit up. I did. He showed me the picture of the girl again. Carefully this time.

"Her name's Theresa Marrero."

"I know her name," I said. "Her first name, anyway."

"She's a big-time snitch. Do anything, say anything a cop wants if it means she gets her deal. And she's good at it."

"How did you know about her?"

"You mean how did I know about her and you? I didn't."

"Then how?"

"Actually, Z put it together. When she heard about your arrest, she suggested I pull a month's worth of booking sheets for Coursey. Theresa was the third name we pulled. Coursey popped her for felony possession three weeks ago. Yesterday he told the prosecutor he didn't think the case was gonna go anywhere and got the charges dropped. We grabbed the jacket on Marrero and found out she'd been hired at the Street Ministry. James Harrison's old stomping grounds."

"And you figured I'd met her there?"

"I showed you the picture. You told me the rest."

I took another sip of Sprite and watched the can shake.

"What happened?" Rodriguez said.

Moncata had stopped cleaning. The detective waited patiently.

"I met her at the Street Ministry," I said. "Ran into her again at a bar in Evanston two nights ago. Maybe it was three since I don't really know what day it is."

"The Fourth of July?" Rodriguez said.

I nodded. "We went back to my place."

"Did you use a condom?" Moncata said. He'd found a plastic pitcher somewhere and was filling it with water.

"To be honest, I don't remember."

Moncata put the pitcher on the table, along with a couple of glasses. "How many drinks did you have, Ian?"

"Three beers. Maybe four. Some tequila later on."

"And you don't remember a thing?" Rodriguez said.

"She might have dropped something in his drink," Moncata said and turned back to me. "She had sex with you, son. Used a condom and harvested the semen. Then she gave it to Coursey."

"They figured they'd wait until the time was right and set you up for something," Rodriguez said. "You gave them their chance by hanging around Sarah Gold's house at two in the morning."

"Can they do that?" I said. "I mean, would it work?"

"If Coursey has your semen," Moncata said, "he could theoretically 'find' it anytime he wanted. On any piece of evidence. It would certainly be enough to get you arrested."

"Which means," Rodriguez said, "that Coursey owns you. At least for the time being."

"Then why hasn't he charged me?"

Rodriguez scratched an ear and shrugged. "Probably because he knows I pulled the booking sheets on Marrero. And he's thinking I might be able to blow it all up. Besides, Coursey doesn't necessarily need you in a cell right now. Just worried you might be."

"Wait a minute," I said. "If they set me up to take the fall . . ."

Rodriguez saw the dark light flick on in my eyes and nodded. "That's right, Ian. If they framed you with Marrero, they also broke into Sarah's apartment and assaulted her. Either Coursey himself. Or one of his cronies."

"It was Coursey," Moncata said. "Fucking guy would love that."

"They take care of you and Sarah with one move," Rodriguez said. "And your little seminar is cooked."

I knew it was true. And knew we were caught. Myself and Sarah. In a web I'd constructed for the two of us. Moncata must have read it on my face.

"You won't go down for this," the scientist said. "If they did decide to prosecute, there are things we could do to attack the forensics."

"I can't go to prison," I said.

"It would only be until you make bail." Moncata gestured toward Rodriguez. "And the detective here could get you protective custody."

"You don't understand." Then I told them about Brian Hines. And how he had James Harrison and the other two killed inside. Rodriguez wrote down Hines's name in a small black book.

"Hines is dead," I said. "But I'm sure they have others who can do the job."

"You're not going to jail," Rodriguez said. "Not even for a night. Sam?"

Moncata stood and stretched. "Time for an old man to get some sleep." He patted me on the shoulder and shook my hand. "I'm sure we'll be seeing each other again."

I watched him leave and wondered if that wasn't my last friend in the room. "Where's he going?"

"There's a guy I want you to meet," Rodriguez said. "He's not with the police. And sometimes he pushes things a little bit. But he's a guy I'd trust with my life."

"Why can't Sam meet him?"

"For right now it's better if it just stays between us. No Sam. No Z. All right?"

"Do I have a choice?"

"Not really."

I was alone for a few minutes, just me and the corpse cooling on the slab a few feet away. Then the door opened and Rodriguez was back with his friend.

"Ian, I'd like you to meet Michael Kelly."

He was a shade under six feet. About a hundred and eighty pounds. Irish, with curly black hair, and blue eyes—scarred at the edges, but still cool and smooth in the center. He wore jeans and a loose gray T-shirt. His shoulders were wide, and he had the hands and arms of a boxer. There was a gun clipped to his hip.

"Hello, Ian."

"Hi . . ."

"Call me Kelly."

"Hi, Kelly."

"You okay with all of this?" His voice was softer than he looked, with a trace of Galway in it.

"I'm not sure I have a choice," I said.

Kelly seemed amused by the answer but didn't respond. He took a seat, clasped his hands behind his head, and kicked a pair of New Balance 902s onto Sam Moncata's recently polished table. Rodriguez waited for his friend to settle in, then turned back to me.

"Here's the plan, Ian. I have to work the two fresh murders for the next day or so. Sam's gonna run the bite-mark evidence with the feds, and we have a couple of local things I need to check out. Meanwhile, Kelly's going to stash you somewhere. The idea is if Coursey can't find you, he can't arrest you. I'll have someone pick up Havens as well."

"What about the cover-up?" I said. "We've got the citric acid on Harrison. We can do something with that."

"Let me deal with the hot homicides first," Rodriguez said. "Sam's got the Harrison evidence under lock and key. We'll play that card when the time is right."

"So Jake and I just hide?" I said.

Rodriguez looked at Kelly, who didn't seem to know how to blink, then back to me.

"What is it?" I said.

"We need to talk about Jake," Rodriguez said.

"What about him?"

Rodriguez leaned forward, hands loose, elbows resting on his knees. "How much do you know about him?"

"How much do I need to know?"

Kelly kicked his feet off the table and poured a glass of water from the pitcher Moncata had left out. Rodriguez kept talking.

"You know about his childhood?"

"His brother drowned. So did mine."

"How about law school?"

"How about it?"

"Jake was involved in some clinical work while he was in law school. He worked with kids in Juvie Court. Got involved in a bad case. A mom who killed two of her kids and was about to do the same to a third. The court didn't see it that way. Said the first two deaths were accidents and put the kid back with the mom. Jake didn't like that."

"What did he do?"

"He showed up at the house and tried to take the boy by force. The mom offered to sell him the kid. When that didn't work, she called the police. It all got settled. Mom's doing twenty on a drug beef and the kid's in a foster home. But . . ."

"But what?" My mouth was suddenly parched. Kelly handed me the water I thought he'd poured for himself. I took a sip and tried to give it back.

"Keep it," Kelly said.

"We're concerned," Rodriguez said. "Incident like that in law school. Before that the trauma with his brother. Now he pops up in the middle of a case where more kids have been killed."

"What are you saying, Detective?"

"He thinks your friend Jake might be a little unstable," Kelly said. "Might be looking to take the law into his own hands if we ever find this guy."

"Never happen," I said and thought about Jake's altercation with Sarah's ex in Nevin's. The pictures of dead children on his bedroom walls. The hard anger in his voice.

"You don't have to believe it," Kelly said. "What the detective wants is for you to be aware."

"Aware of what?"

"The situation," Rodriguez said. "Kelly's gonna check on a few things about Jake while the three of you are together. Hang around a little and observe. Look, I'm not saying Jake's gonna hurt anybody. Or anything like that. I just wanted you to know. And be warned. Okay?"

I pulled my eyes off my shoes and took a look around the room. There were no easy answers to be found. And I was out of options.

"One condition," I said and held up a finger.

"What's that?" Rodriguez said.

"I want to see Sarah."

39

The room was small, the couch, uncomfortable, and there was at least one body in the freezer next door. Still, I slept the sleep of the dead in the Cook County Morgue. And didn't mind the irony a bit. Rodriguez woke me at just after eight. We didn't talk much on the drive to Northwestern Memorial Hospital. He insisted on speaking to Sarah first. When he came out, he had a tight look on his face.

"How is she?" I said.

"She's fine. I caught her up on most of what we talked about."

"Including who actually attacked her?"

"Yeah. Believe it or not, Coursey's been in to see her twice. Working the case."

"What if he finds out I'm here?"

"That's why we have to hustle. Ten minutes, no more. And if anyone ever asks down the road, the whole thing never happened."

"Is there anything I should tell her?"

"Something that's gonna make her feel better would be nice."

She was sitting up in bed, like she had the flu, except one eye was mostly shut, her lip was split, and a bruise in twisted shades of yellow and purple ran down one cheek and along her jaw.

"Does it hurt to talk?" I said.

"Not too bad." Her voice sounded brittle, almost afraid of itself. I decided to cut my ten minutes to five.

"How long are you going to be in?"

"They're supposed to let me out tomorrow."

I looked around. The room was bare, with just a spray of flowers in a vase by the door. "Is your family coming down?"

"My mom and dad are coming in today. I didn't tell them until last night. Couldn't deal with all the drama."

I moved a little closer. "Listen, I just wanted to say I'm sorry . . ."

She shook her head and opened her arms. I held her close and felt her bones under the hospital gown.

"Sarah . . ."

"Don't talk about it."

"I was there that night. I shouldn't have been, but I was. They set me up. Set us up."

"I know what they did. And I know why."

"You don't think I attacked you?"

A fragile smile peeked through the catalog of bruises. "Never did." She settled her head against my chest. My fingers found the pulse along her wrist. I sat on the edge of the bed and counted heartbeats.

"You remember the volunteer work I told you about? Helping women who've been abused?" Her voice was low and muffled, like she was in a confessional.

"Sure."

She looked up. "I'm on the other side of that now. And I need to be strong."

"I got you covered, Sarah. Whichever way it goes."

"That's what I told Rodriguez. I think he liked that." She leaned back into me and we sat in the cool darkness of the hospital room. I thought she might have drifted off when she spoke again. "I've got something for you." She reached down to the side of her bed for a thick manila envelope.

"What is it?"

"Something I was working on before everything happened. Detective Rodriguez brought it down from my apartment. I thought it could wait, but maybe you should have it now."

"Sarah . . ."

"Jake filled me in on the Needle Squad. Told me you thought the two core members were dead."

"Teddy Green and John Carlton."

Sarah shoved the envelope into my hands. "Read through this." There was a light knock on the door. "We can catch up on the rest later."

I tucked the envelope under my arm. "Are you gonna be all right?"

"That probably depends on what you mean by 'all right.'" A hard light came into her eyes. "Detective Coursey was in here last night. He said he needed to see my bruises, and I let him touch me. Just so he wouldn't become suspicious."

"I'm sorry."

"If that man attacked me, I need to know. And I need for him to pay. Whoever did this needs to pay in a court of law. Can you understand that?"

"I think so."

"Good." The anger softened and Sarah Gold was suddenly, inexpressibly old. She spread her fingers and held her palm flat against mine. "There's no going back, Ian. Not for me. Not for any of us." She paused, giving me room to speak, but I didn't. There was another small knock on the door. "You better get going."

I leaned in and kissed her cheek. It was as cool as clay. I lingered another minute, then shoved the manila envelope under my shirt and headed for the door. On the way out, I took a look at the card on the flowers. They were from Jake.

I told Rodriguez I needed a minute, went into the bathroom, and pulled out Sarah's envelope. Clipped inside were old lab reports on blood typing from the Wingate and Allen murders and hair and fiber analyses from the Scranton case. A different expert had testified in each trial, but the actual work had been done by one forensic scientist. Sarah had highlighted the analyst's name on each of the old reports. SALLY FINN. Sarah had also included a few newspaper clippings. They traced the rise of Finn from lab tech to chief of the Cook County lab in 1994 and then head of the Illinois State Police lab until her retirement in 2005. Sarah had highlighted Finn's name again in one of the articles and written beside it in capital letters: THIRD CORE MEMBER— NEEDLE SQUAD??

I slid Sarah's documents into the envelope and stuffed it back under my shirt. Rodriguez was waiting in the hallway. He took me down in the elevator and out a side entrance. Kelly sat behind the wheel of a car idling in the alley. Rodriguez shoved me into the front seat without a word, and Kelly pulled away. Two unmarked cars, flashers rolling, pulled up in front of the hospital. I ducked down in the front seat as Coursey climbed out of one and disappeared through the revolving doors. Then we were gone.

40

Kelly cruised north on Lake Shore Drive.

"Where are we headed?" I said.

"The Willows Hotel. Used to be called the Surf. You know it?"

"No."

"It's where they kept Richard Speck during his trial. Killed eight nurses back in the day."

"Is that supposed to be funny?"

"You'll have to ask Rodriguez, but I don't think he has much of a sense of humor these days."

Kelly got off at Fullerton and headed up Cannon Drive.

"Can I ask how this is going to work?" I said.

"How what's gonna work?"

I flapped my hands at nothing. "This. Whatever it is Rodriguez wants you to do."

Kelly glanced over. "Fuck Rodriguez. What is it you want to do?"

"Seriously?"

"Uh-huh."

"I want to go after the pricks who attacked Sarah. Framed three innocent men. And then had them killed in prison."

"The Needle Squad? Or what's left of it?"

"You know them?" I said.

"I used to be a cop. They were the big guns. Never let anyone work on their cases, except for their people."

"Now we know why," I said.

"You think so?"

"Don't you?"

"Who is it you want to go after?"

"Who do you think? Coursey."

Kelly shook his head. "I know Marty Coursey. Dumb as a fucking doorknob. Kind of looks like one, too."

"You're saying he's not involved?"

"I'd say he's behind the attack on your friend, if that's what you're after." A pause. "But he's not the one behind it all."

We'd barely driven two miles and already Kelly had me thinking, reconsidering. I'd have to keep an eye on him.

"Who then?" I said.

He shrugged. "Most of 'em are dead. Lead prosecutor. Chief of detectives. But someone's out there. And they got something cooking. Something worth protecting."

I thought about dropping the name of Sally Finn but decided I'd keep it to myself for now. We clipped past Diversey, swung a left onto Oakdale, and came around the block to Surf Street. Kelly found a spot in front of a hydrant.

"Your buddy's in room 302. I put you next door." He tossed over a key card.

"What about you?" I said.

"Don't worry. I'll be around."

"So you're all right with us going after these guys?"

"First, you need to figure out exactly who 'these guys' are. But why not? I mean, who else will?"

"What about Rodriguez?"

"Let me worry about him."

"He said you two were friends. Said he'd trust you with his life."

"Rodriguez is a romantic. It's the Latino in him."

"Is it true?"

"You wondering if you can trust me?"

"Do I have a choice?"

"Not really. Going after Coursey alone might get you killed. Then again, doing nothing might get you killed."

"So you think they'll come after us?"

"They already have."

"What about the FBI or something?"

"What about them?"

"We can turn over the evidence we have and let them start an investigation."

"Is that what you want to do?" His words were clipped. The silence that followed appraised without judging.

"I don't know," I said.

"I wouldn't look to the feds for protection. Not in Chicago."

"What are you saying?"

"What Rodriguez wants to say but can't. You got yourself into something. Get yourself out."

"I think that's what Sarah was trying to tell me."

"Smart woman."

"I'm not sure I could kill anyone," I said and felt a dry patch at the back of my throat. "I mean, if I had to."

"Follow the evidence. Let me worry about the guys with the guns."

"So I *can* trust you?"

"I'd worry more about ability than trust, but let's hope it doesn't come to that. Speaking of killing, we haven't talked about your buddy in there. Jake."

"What about him?"

"You don't agree with Rodriguez? About Jake looking to drop the hammer on someone?"

"Jake's not a killer either."

"I think you might be right."

I blinked.

"You look surprised," Kelly said.

"I am."

"Cops make mistakes, too. Even cops as good as Rodriguez."

"How about you?"

"All the time. I'd suggest you keep your friend on a loose leash. At least until I look into a few things. Now get out of here. I've got places to be."

And then I was standing in the street, watching Michael Kelly drive away. I walked down the block to the Willows. Jake Havens was sitting on the front porch, peering at me through a stand of trees.

41

"How did you get here?" I said and sat down beside him.

"Z."

"She call you?"

"She met me at the hospital. Drove up here with me."

I thought about Jake Havens, sitting in the same corridor I'd just left. Standing by Sarah's bed.

"What did Z tell you?" I said.

"That we should hole up here and quit digging around the Wingate case."

"What about the rest?"

"Rodriguez filled me in on the cop. Coursey. Said if I wanted any details, I should ask you." Havens bit off the last few words and looked like he wanted to punch me in the jaw.

"I didn't touch her, Jake."

"Rodriguez believes it."

"How about you?"

"She told me about you and her on the beach."

"It was nothing."

"You think I care? Why were you stalking her?"

"I wasn't . . ."

"Really? What do you call sitting in your car, in front of her apartment, in the middle of the night?"

"I'm sorry, Jake."

"Don't be. Just convince me I can trust you."

"I don't know how I can do that."

A couple came out of the front door of the hotel and turned up Surf toward Broadway.

"They asked me for a DNA sample," Havens said, "which means they took samples from Sarah's body."

I looked at the ground and kicked at a rock that wasn't there.

"I told them I wasn't with her," Havens said, "and I wasn't."

"The DNA's gonna come back as a match to me," I said.

"I know. Rodriguez explained it all."

"Do you believe him?"

Nothing.

"Would I be that stupid, Jake? Do I seem that stupid?"

"So your semen found at a rape is proof you didn't do it?"

"I guess so."

"Fucking great." Havens shook his head, and we sat for a while. I felt nothing but shame. And it humbled me.

"Sarah got in my head," I said. "The two of you got in my head."

"You stalked us, Joyce."

"I didn't touch her."

"Jesus Christ."

"What do you want me to say?" At the end of the day he was either going to help me or not. And I needed to find out which. "Did Rodriguez tell you about the citric acid?"

"He told me."

"What do you think?"

"I think we got them."

"That's right, Jake. We got them. And that's why they attacked Sarah and framed me. Because they're scared."

"They've been scared all along."

"Yeah, well, they've upped the ante big time. Have you met Kelly?"

"He's supposed to protect us or something."

"No one's gonna be able to protect us. They know we're onto something, and they're gonna do what they do. Arrest us. Frame us.

Kill us. And if we decide to disappear for a while, they'll wait. We can't live our lives in the Willows."

Havens seemed surprised by the aggressive attitude, but willing. "What do you have in mind?"

"Do you trust me?"

"I don't trust you, but I believe you. About Sarah, anyway."

It wasn't all I wanted, but it would have to do. "I've got an idea of how the Needle Squad worked. Who might be behind this. And what they might be trying to protect."

"So?"

"So we go for it. Get them before they get us. If nothing else, we get them for Sarah." I showed him the envelope of information she'd given me on Sally Finn.

"So you want to try to find this woman, Finn?"

"Not yet," I said.

"I'm not following you."

"We need to start with the first link in the food chain."

"And who would that be?"

"Come on. I'll explain on the way."

42

"Z?" Havens glanced across at me. He'd stashed his car three blocks from the Willows. Now we were driving north on Lake Shore Drive, headed toward Evanston.

"She's the first link in the chain."

"How?"

"My brother drowned on the Fourth of July. Every year I visit his grave in Evanston, just as the cemetery opens. I was there again this year."

"Three days ago?"

"That's right. I saw one other person that morning in the graveyard. Dressed in black."

"Z?"

"She was standing in front of a headstone. I couldn't get too close, but it looked like she was crying. After she left, I got the name on the marker." I took out a piece of paper and slapped it on the dashboard. "Rosina Rolland. Born October 3, 1972. Died July 4, 1992."

"I don't get it."

"Neither did I. After the cemetery, I did a Nexis search for Rolland. Turns out she died in a late-night car crash on an access road feeding onto the Edens."

"Let me guess. She was drunk."

"Hardly. Rosina worked at an all-night IHOP just off the highway. She was in her uniform when the EMTs pulled her out of the car."

"So what?"

"So why is Z mourning the death of a kid from the South Side of Chicago?"

"Maybe she was a relative?"

"Rosina Rolland was black."

"Oh."

"Did you know Z took a medical leave of absence from work? More than a year, from July of '92 through August of '93. I couldn't find any explanation why."

Havens was off the Drive and heading north on Sheridan. "What are you getting at?"

"Pull over."

Havens cruised under the Loyola stop on the Red Line and pulled into a parking lot for a burger joint. I took a folder full of photos out of my pack.

"What are those?" Havens said.

"Rosina Rolland's dad gave them to me. They're from the accident."

Havens flipped through the shots. Rolland's car was on its roof. The entire front left side was caved in.

"Rosina's dad has his doubts about whether this was a one-person accident," I said. "When you look at the car, you can see why."

"Who handled the scene?" Havens said.

"Chicago police. The accident was off the highway and just inside the city limits. Rosina's dad also gave me this."

I handed over a copy of the original police report. The chicken scratch was hard to read, but the cop's name typed at the bottom was clear enough. MARTIN J. COURSEY.

"Someone hit Rosina Rolland and killed her," I said. "They called Coursey, and he came out to clean up the mess."

"And you think . . ."

"I think that someone was Z. And the Needle Squad has owned her ever since."

She lived in a Queen Anne–style home, a few blocks from the university. We had agreed that I would take the lead. Other than that, there wasn't too much of a plan. I rang her bell. The front door opened almost immediately.

"What are you two doing here?" She took a quick look down the block and swept us inside. The living room was as cold as a tomb—tiled floors, purple orchids, and furniture made from leather and steel. She sat us on a hard-as-a-rock couch. I stared at a black-and-white print of a man screaming as skin melted off the bones of his face.

"Stay here," she said and left.

I could hear the tinkle of ice in glasses. Z returned with a tray of soft drinks. We each took one, even though we hadn't asked for anything. Z sat in a chair across from us. She gripped and regripped the cold glass as she spoke.

"Why aren't you down at the Willows? And where's Rodriguez?"

"He's working a case," I said.

"Did he not explain . . ."

"He explained everything. We just didn't feel like waiting around."

Z jumped to her feet, shoes clicking on the floor as she paced. "I don't think you realize the situation you've put yourselves in. The situation you've put me in."

"We do," I said.

Z stopped pacing and turned. Her face was choked with color. A bead of moisture hung on her upper lip. "I don't think you do."

"We came here to talk about Rosina Rolland," Havens said.

Z dropped into her chair like she'd been shot. She reached for her drink and then moved her hands back into her lap. "Excuse me?"

"Rosina Rolland," I said. "You killed her twenty years ago. On the Fourth of July."

"I've never heard of Rosina Rolland."

"I saw you," I said. "At Calvary Cemetery."

Z pulled out a cell phone and began to dial. "I'm going to call the detective. You both need to get back to the Willows."

"They already raped Sarah, and they want to put him in jail for it," Havens said, jerking a thumb my way.

"That's why you gave Rodriguez the tip on Theresa Marrero," I said. "You knew I was being set up and didn't want to see it happen."

"Maybe they'll just kill us next," Havens said. "If you can't stomach a rape, what are you going to do with that?"

"We'll leave if you want," I said. "You can wait here and see how it all turns out. Or you can help us. And maybe get your life back."

She took us up to a locked room in an attic on the third floor of her house. The room was empty except for an old-fashioned wooden desk, a few chairs, and three battered metal cabinets. A small window looked out on a square of white light.

"This is where I work sometimes," Z said. "Please, sit down."

She pulled out a set of keys and fitted one into the bottom drawer of the middle cabinet. The drawer creaked open. Z took out a red accordion folder.

"I keep some of my old pieces in here. As well as any other stories I feel might be important." Z pulled out a stack of clippings held together with a paper clip. On top was a blurry picture of Rosina Rolland and a small blurb about the accident.

"I was twenty-eight," she said. "A city reporter. Good, but not great. I'd been on an all-day boat cruise. A party that left from Lake Bluff. Had six or seven drinks and never should have driven home. Goddamnit, I never should have driven." Z dropped her head so all I could see was the part in her hair and white scalp. She rocked back and forth and rubbed her fingers over the dead girl's face as she talked.

"I never even knew I was off the highway. I think I must have taken the exit ramp by mistake. All of a sudden I was on a small access road. Going way too fast. There was a dip in the pavement and some dirt flying up, hitting the windshield. The car skidded and I wound up in a ditch." She looked at me. Then Jake. Our professor was on trial. And we were her jury. "All I could think of was a cop coming by. Blowing a two point three or something. The publicity. My career. So I gunned the engine, got out of the ditch, and beelined for the highway. I had it in my head that I needed to get back on the Edens. Blend in with all the other Fourth of July drunks. I never saw Rosina."

She stopped talking and stared at the photo. I glanced at Havens, who gestured that I should keep quiet.

"Afterward, I was banged up pretty bad. I still don't know what possessed me to call Coursey. That's bullshit. I know. We got drunk one night a year earlier, and I screwed him in the back of his car. Okay?"

We didn't respond. I didn't think she much cared anymore. If she ever had, that is.

"Anyway, I knew him. Knew he was connected. Could fix things downtown. He was up there in ten minutes. God knows how, but he stuck me in a car. Someone drove me to a hospital. And that's all I know. Never talked about it again."

"But you heard from Coursey?" Havens said.

"I figured it would be sex. A quickie whenever he wanted. If only." Z pulled out another set of clippings. "This was the first time."

I picked up a front-page story under Z's byline and dated November 4, 1993. The headline read: GONE TO THE DOGS? The picture was of a vacant lot sitting under the tracks near the Addison L stop. An inset featured the smiling, sweating face of a man named Manny Silva.

"You wouldn't remember this story," Z said. "Silva was a Chicago alderman. He used his cousin as a straw man and bought two parcels of property for next to nothing near Wrigley. Then Silva used his clout to get a zoning variance that would allow him to open up a hot-dog stand at the location. Coursey tipped me off about the story. Told me Silva was dirty and told me exactly where to look."

"So what?" I said. "If Silva was doing something illegal, he should be exposed."

Z shook her head. "Silva was set up from the start. The seller fed him the property, told Silva about the hot-dog-stand idea, even gave him plans for the build out. After I 'exposed' Silva, the sale was rescinded and the property returned to the original seller, who later sold it to the city for three times what it was worth. And I got my first look at how this thing worked. They'd target someone they wanted to get rid of, someone like Manny Silva. Then they'd give me the story, and I'd run it."

"And no one would ever hear about Rosina Rolland," Havens said.

Z pulled out another article and slipped it onto the desk.

"You probably recognize this one. I was teaching the seminar but still working at the *Trib*."

The year was 1999. Z had uncovered a sex scandal involving Illinois's sitting lieutenant governor. Married and a "family values" guy, he'd managed to get himself tangled up with a college intern. Z had been in their hip pocket from the beginning. Photos of romantic dinners at the taxpayers' expense. Out-of-town trips. The intern heading into the lieutenant governor's Atlanta hotel one evening. Coming out wearing the same clothes the next morning. Z had it all nailed. Still shots. Receipts. Reimbursement requests billed to the taxpayers. The lieutenant governor resigned a week after the story broke. His wife left him a day later. The man returned to Peoria and his former career as a pharmacist.

"The intern was another plant," Z said. "A good-looking, very experienced college kid they paid to target the lieutenant governor and seduce him. She documented all of it, then passed it along to me."

"What did she get out of it?" Havens said.

"The girl wanted to go to law school, but her grades were awful. Her LSAT scores were worse. After this story broke, she reapplied and was accepted to three of the top seven schools in the country. Same grades. Same LSATs. Now she's a major lobbyist for a dozen tech firms out of the Midwest. Pulls down half a million a year and gives lectures to college-aged women about how she was victimized and ways to avoid making the same mistakes."

"Why the lieutenant governor?" I said.

"I never asked why. Over the years, there were maybe a dozen stories I did for Coursey. Each was a setup. A way to destroy someone or something. One might be a downstate scam. The next in DuPage County. Then something in Chicago."

"Never any pattern to the victims?" I said.

"I thought the same thing," Z said. "Figure out who's benefiting and at least I'll know who's pulling the strings. But it just wasn't there. At least not that I could see."

"But you got a career out of it," Havens said.

Z raised her chin. "We're talking about a handful of stories. The rest were my own, including three Pulitzers that had nothing to do with Coursey."

"What about Billy Scranton's murder?" I said. "You won a Pulitzer for that."

"So what?"

"Scranton was killed by the same guy who killed Skylar Wingate. The guy the Needle Squad convicted was framed. But you already know that. Hell, you helped frame him."

I could see Z's eyes working back and forth, like she was adding up numbers in her head. "They told me the guy was guilty as hell. Told me I was taking a killer off the street."

"And you bought it?" Havens said.

"I'm not going to be judged by you two." Z stuffed the clippings back in the folder and put it all away. "I told you. They owned me."

"I don't believe you," I said.

Z chuckled. "Like I give a damn."

"The men who ran the Needle Squad are dead. So who's in charge now?"

"I dealt with Coursey. That's it."

"Where would you start then?" Havens said. "If you were us?"

"They really will kill you," she said. "You understand that?"

"Where would you start?"

Z moistened her lips with the tip of her tongue. "The fact that there's no pattern to the targets tells you something."

I leaned forward. "What?"

"At some point the folks behind this graduated from framing innocent men and advancing their careers to doing it for hire."

"You mean for money?"

"Or some sort of favor. In either case, it's absolutely work for hire."

"Who would it be?" Havens said.

Z went back to her pile of clippings and dug out a *Chicago* magazine article from the Needle Squad's heyday. She put a red fingernail on a picture of a woman who bore a striking resemblance to the Wicked Witch of the West. And that was with a fair wind. Her name was Sally Finn.

"We know about Finn," I said.

Our professor nodded her head in appreciation. "Very good. You both get an A. She was the third key member of the Needle Squad. Low profile. And the only one still alive."

"She's retired," I said. "And she's got to be well into her seventies."

"Sally Finn is smarter than anyone in this room, and that includes you, Havens. Not to mention she's a fire-breathing, subzero bitch. I don't know for a fact, but she's got to be involved."

"Where does she live?" Havens said.

"After she left the state lab, she disappeared."

"You wouldn't tell us about her if you didn't have an idea."

Z picked up a pen and scratched out an address on a piece of paper. "She lives alone. Never married. No kids. This was the last address I ever got for her. About an hour and a half from here, in Michigan."

"You ever been up there?" I said.

"I don't know anyone who's been up there," Z said. "If you knew Sally Finn, you'd understand why."

43

Neither of us commented on it, but we both felt it. An urgency to get some answers before the hourglass emptied and the past caught up with our present. Maybe it would be a set of cuffs and a jail cell. Maybe they'd just kill us. Maybe both. And so we pressed on, the specter of Coursey looming in our rearview mirror as we pounded down the Indiana tollway toward Michigan.

Finn lived in a small wooded area just north of a small town called Bridgman. Her house was planted on a cliff overlooking Lake Michigan. Jake and I parked a mile away and walked up the beach to have a look.

"How much you think that goes for?" Havens said.

The house was old, its white façade long since scoured gray by the weather. A single turret spiked into the sky, and a set of stairs wound down to an empty beach. There was a dock built out onto the water. A twenty-foot Whaler was tethered at the end.

"Whatever it costs, she can afford it," I said. "Come on, let's talk."

We found a spot a quarter mile down the beach and sat in the sand. The sun was ducking in and out of cloud cover, and there was a freshening breeze that held the promise of rain. I looked out over the rollers. Chicago's skyline shimmered in a light haze, fifty miles away.

"So, what do we do?" Havens said.

"We get inside."

He snorted and threw a rock at the water. "Just like that."

"You think Finn's still involved in all of this?" I said.

"Sarah thinks so. So does Z."

"Z's guessing," I said.

"Or lying."

"I don't think Finn has anything to do with what's going on in Chicago," I said.

"Then why are we here?"

"Because she's the only one left from the original group. She might have some answers about what happened after the Needle Squad disbanded. And she might be willing to talk."

Havens picked up another rock. This time he threw it at a seagull who was staring at us from atop a piece of driftwood. "Let me guess. You want to walk up there and knock on her front door."

"I was thinking more of the back door. Or maybe an open window."

"It's called breaking and entering, Joyce."

"Come on."

We hiked up the stairs, taking shelter in a copse of trees that ran out along the edge of the property line. The house looked worse the closer we got to it. The porch steps were broken, and one of the railings had fallen into the backyard. There was a line of hedges on either side of the house and a hammock was tied off between two trees.

"What do you see?" I said.

"An old house with a beat-up back porch."

"I'm guessing we could jimmy that open." I pointed to a small ground-level window halfway down one side of the house.

"With what?" Havens said. "And why?"

Just then the back door banged open, and a woman came out. She was wearing oversize, dark sunglasses and a broad-brimmed hat with a shock of white hair underneath. She was tall and bent. Her teeth flashed in the sun.

The woman pulled sunscreen from a flowered bag, squirted a good amount into her hands, and worked it into the loose, pebbly skin that hung in folds off her neck and arms. When she was done, she put the lotion away, picked up the bag, and started down a path that ran along the side of the house. The woman disappeared between a gap in the hedges.

"Come on," Havens said.

We crept down the path and peered into a cove constructed of landscaped bushes and trees. A steel shed sat in the very center. The woman was standing beside the door. It popped open, and she disappeared inside. Havens rushed forward, but the door closed well before he got to it. There was a large generator on one side of the shed and what looked like a heavy-duty AC unit. Havens pointed to a set of power lines crossing overhead.

"Two hundred twenty volts."

We made our way back toward the front of the shed. Jake touched me at the shoulder and gestured toward a keypad by the door.

"What is it?" I said, one eye on the door, waiting for it to swing open.

"The keypad," Havens said and moved closer.

The pad contained buttons numbered zero to thirty. Four of the numbers were smeared with bits of white sunscreen. Havens grinned and pointed to a # symbol at the very bottom. It, too, had a dab of white on it.

We snuck back down the path. I was tempted to take a chance on the house, but Havens pulled me into the tree line. Smart move as the woman in the hat appeared on the path less than two minutes later. She went back into the house. Twenty minutes after that, the garage door opened and a Lexus pulled out. The woman was in the front seat, alone. We watched her drive away.

"I think that was Finn," Havens said.

"Has to be," I said. "What about the shed?"

"You get the numbers?"

I nodded.

"Can you do it?"

"I can try."

"Let's take a look."

Assuming no numbers were repeated, four digits and a # symbol generated one hundred and twenty possible combinations. I sat against the wall of the shed, closed my eyes, and lined up the numbers in my head. Havens stood by the keypad, waiting.

"You ready?" I said.

"Fuck, yeah."

I read a combination off the inside of my eyelids. Havens punched it in. Nothing. I gave him another. Still nothing. I could hear the rush and suck of the waves as they hit the beach below us. Otherwise, my world was quiet. Just Jake's voice. Asking for another number. Then a fourth. Combination thirty-eight proved to be the charm. The door to the shed popped open, and we stepped inside.

It was dark. A current of cold air dried the sweat on my chest and raised the hair on my arms. Havens found a light switch and turned on the overheads. We were standing in a room that could have only belonged to a scientist. A countertop of black granite ran the length of the facing wall. Above it, a row of blond-wood cabinets. Two deep sinks of stainless steel sat in equipoise at either end of the counter. In between was a row of test tubes, a rack of pipettes, a computer monitor, and three microscopes in front of three stools. From somewhere to our left came the soft thump and groan of a compressor.

"Come on," Havens said.

We found our way into a small, adjoining room. A walk-in cooler took up half the space. Beside it was a row of three black cabinets. We moved closer to the walk-in. It, too, was locked, with another keypad set just above the handle. This one, unfortunately, wasn't covered in sunscreen.

"What do you think?" Havens said.

I punched in the numbers from the front door. Nothing. I dropped off the # symbol. More nothing.

"Try reversing them," Havens said.

"Why?"

"Just try it. And put the symbol back in."

I did. The door popped open.

"Scientists," Havens said. "No fucking imagination."

We pushed into the cooler and a small light clicked on. The space was filled with long, low metal racks—each containing as many as ten to fifteen test tubes. I picked up a tube filled with a yellowish liquid and looked at the tag on it.

SUBJECT 26D
8/25/06
SEMEN . . . NO EXPIRATION DATE

"What do you think?" I said.
"Pretty fucked up."
"That's it?"
"I think semen dies within a few hours after it's ejaculated."
"How about its DNA signature?" I said. "Planted at a crime scene?"
Havens picked up another vial. The tag read:

SUBJECT 3B
BLOOD . . . COLLECTION DATE 2010 ** SEE SUBJECT'S CHART.

Havens placed the tube back in its rack. "I got an idea." He walked out of the cooler and over to the black cabinets. "These guys are locked with a key."

"What are you looking for?" I said.

"There's gotta be a chart that decodes what's in the cooler. And who belongs to what. How long have we been in there?"

"About five minutes."

"We've got time."

Havens ran out of the shed, back along the path, to the main house. The door on the back porch was locked. A small window next to it was cracked an inch. We jacked it open and squeezed through. The living room was large and shabby, with a long velvet couch at one end, two matching chairs, and a couple of bare tables. No pictures anywhere, no sign of life except for a cat who meowed at us from atop a mantel. Havens passed through the living room and walked down the hallway. I followed him to a small study. A metal desk took up nearly the entire room.

"Gotta be here," Havens said.

"What?"

"I told you. Finn's a scientist. No imagination. So she either has the keys with her or leaves them in her house. In fact, I bet she does both."

Havens dug through the desk. In the bottom left-hand drawer he found a small ring of keys and dangled them in front of me. "What do you think?"

"Worth a try."

"Damn straight."

We sprinted back down the path and into the shed. Everything seemed as we left it. Havens tried a couple of keys in one of the cabinet locks. The third one turned easily, and the door slid open.

"Fuck me," Havens said. I crowded closer. The filing cabinet was filled with videotapes, stored on shelves and labeled by subject matter:

DEATHS (INCLUDING DUIs, ACCIDENTS, MURDER)
RAPE (INCLUDING DATE RAPE)
SEX (HOOKERS, WIVES, GIRLFRIENDS, ALL ADULTS)
KIDS

I pulled out one of the tapes from the SEX shelf. It was labeled in much the same manner as the test tubes.

SUBJECT 11A
4/5/98 . . . PONY LOUNGE MOTEL, LOMBARD . . .
THREESOME

There was a creak of wood and metal beside me. Havens had cracked open the second cabinet. It contained more tapes and a stack of brown files marked PHOTOS. On a back shelf, I found a file labeled ZOMBROWSKI, J. I stuffed it under my shirt and looked over at Havens. He had his head deep into the third cabinet.

"Anything?" I said.

"Could be." In the dim light, he held up a Moleskine notebook bound in black. A red label stuck to the front right corner of the notebook read: MASTER. We went back into the main room and sat at the counter. Havens opened up to page 1. The first name I saw was a former Illinois governor and onetime candidate for president. He was listed as SUBJECT 1A. Underneath his name were twenty more. I recognized a sitting U.S. senator from Iowa, SUBJECT 9A, cross referenced under SEX/SEMEN; two Chicago aldermen, SUBJECT 14A and 19A respectively, under DEATH/DUI/BLOOD; and a philanthropist and CEO of a major corporation, SUBJECT 3C, tagged under KIDS/PEDOPHILE/VIDEO.

"You getting all this, memory man?" Havens moved his finger to turn the page. I grabbed the book and closed it.

"What are you doing?" Havens said.

"We can't go through everything here."

"We can take a peek."

"If we're gonna do it, let's do it right."

"What does that mean?"

"I think we need to bring in Rodriguez."

"You trust him?"

"He's about the only one I do trust."

"Hold on." Havens walked back into the other room.

I listened as he rustled around in one of the open cabinets and felt the weight of the leather notebook in my hand. A soft breeze crept up the back of my neck. I turned toward the shed's front door—just in time to catch the glancing blow of a rifle across the temple.

Cold tiles rubbed up against my cheek and a finger pulled back my eyelid. I looked up at the hem of a black dress, a hand holding a pistol, and, finally, a face.

"He's still conscious," Z said and stepped back.

Marty Coursey swam into view. "Remember me?" Coursey raised his rifle high and brought it down again, hard. The last thing I remembered was a gun going off.

44

I woke up a second time on a floor of rough cement, hands and feet cuffed to an iron ring set into a wall. I was in a narrow, dimly lit room. A long window ran just under the rafters and I could hear wind and waves in the night. There was another sound, closer by. Shallow, wet breathing.

"Jake?"

"Over here."

They'd rolled him into the shadows.

"I can't see you," I said.

"You ain't missing much." He tried to laugh, but his voice was thready. For the first time I noticed a dark stain seeping toward a sunken drain in the middle of the floor. It was blood. Jake's blood.

"Did they shoot you?"

"Sort of. I made a run at Coursey when he hit you with the rifle. The old bitch had a gun."

"It was Z," I said.

"What?"

"Z was dressed in the hat and sunglasses. I got a look at her before I went out. How bad is it?"

"She got me in the lower back. I'm bleeding and feel a little dizzy. Z?"

"She's been the brains behind this the whole time. She was the one who told me you were with Sarah that night. Probably hoped I'd do exactly what I did. She was the one who sent us out here. Set us up."

"Why?"

"Because you wouldn't let it be." Z stepped into the light. Her skin was scrubbed to the consistency of rubber and her hair was pulled back from her face. She wore a black rain slicker and green boots. When the slicker opened, I caught the flash of a knife in her belt.

"How bad is he?" she said and pointed in Jake's direction. Coursey was just behind her and moved forward to check.

"He's bleeding pretty good."

Z looked at the puddle on the floor. "Bandage him. And clean up the blood before it gets into the drain."

"You're worried," I said.

"You should have left things alone. I told you that from the beginning." She moved closer and checked my cuffs. Jake let out a small groan as Coursey tugged at him.

"I don't want him dying in here," Z said. Coursey just nodded and kept working.

"When did you start running the show?" I said.

"You mean when did I decide to stop being a victim? They blackmailed me for ten years. During that time, I learned all I could about the operation. Then I just worked my way up. Like any good organization, it takes time. Eventually, however, I got to the top of the food chain. Now, I control the information. People pay for us to stir the sewer. People pay to keep things quiet. Either way, business has never been better."

"We saw your files," I said.

"You'll be at the bottom of the lake within the hour, so it's not a big problem."

"Why did you wait until we were out here?"

She cocked her head. "You should be a lot more scared than you are."

"I'm terrified."

"We'll see. I would have done the deed at my house. Had something nice and easy to slip into your drinks, but we didn't know where Rodriguez was. So I sent you out here. Let you run around until we'd made sure no one followed you out of the city. Then we put you down. For all the headaches you caused, it'll be pretty simple in the end. Tragic boating accident. Your friends might kick and scream, but they'll get over it."

Z took a syringe out of her pocket and unsheathed it. I couldn't take my eyes off the needle.

"Are you going to fight me?" she said.

I wanted to cry, beg, plead, but it wouldn't do any good. I understood now. Or maybe I knew just enough to realize I knew nothing at all.

"Why the graveyard, Z? Why the black dress?"

"I grieved for Rosina Rolland. I still do. I'll grieve for you as well. But what's to be done?"

"Fuck you."

"Perfect." She sank the needle into my arm and watched my eyes.

"Where's the old lady?" I said.

"Finn?" She laughed, her donkey bray rattling around the room. Across the way, Coursey had Jake bandaged and laid up against the wall. His face looked like melted wax, and I wondered if they'd drugged him.

"Why do you care about her?" Z said.

I didn't really know why. Except that it was better than going to sleep.

"She's upstairs in the house," Z said. "Her brain is mush, and she's strapped to a bed. Any other questions?"

My head felt impossibly heavy. I grabbed at a thought, but missed. Another came at me out of the mist. I caught it and shaped it into words.

"Why did you help Rodriguez when I was arrested? Why did you tell him about the girl?"

"Trust." Z turned my hand over and felt for a pulse. I looked at her dumbly. "Give someone like Rodriguez a bone like that, and he trusts you forever. Then he's yours. We call it the Innocence Game. That's why I taught the seminar at Medill. I mean, what better place to be?" She let my arm drop. "Now go to sleep. When you wake up, you'll be on the bottom of Lake Michigan."

45

To my great surprise, I woke up dry and still breathing air. They had me laid up in the bottom of the Whaler I'd seen tied off to the dock. Except now it was moving. My hands were cuffed in front of me. A length of heavy chain was wrapped around my legs and looped through a cleat near the engine. Jake was slumped a few feet away. His cuffs were off, and he was bleeding freely again. I wasn't sure if he was still alive. Not that it mattered much.

It was dark and covered running lights ran down both sides of the boat. A damp fog had crept over the lake, and the bow was shrouded in a yellow mist. Somewhere behind me the engine cut out, and we drifted. Coursey came through the curtain first. He had a rifle in his hands. Z was next. She had the knife out. Wicked and sharp. Coursey handed the rifle to Z and took the blade. Then he squatted over Jake. Like a jackal looking over the remains of someone else's dinner.

"Let him go," I said. "He didn't see anything."

"Shut up." Coursey looked back at Z. "I thought they were both supposed to be out?"

"We went a little farther offshore than I intended. Just stick to your business."

"Please." I reached out. Z held the rifle in front of her with both hands.

"Don't," she said. "Not now."

"I should put some more holes in him," Coursey said, pointing to Jake's side. "Make sure he goes right down."

"That's why we came out so far," Z said. "So we wouldn't have to worry about anything washing up."

Jake groaned. The bottom of the boat was slick with his blood.

"I like to be sure," Coursey said.

"Just put him over."

Coursey sized Z up but decided not to take her on. Not today, anyway. He ripped the last bits of tape off Jake's back. Then he dragged him over to the side of the boat. The wind blew Coursey's hair back, revealing a bald pate covered with black freckles. He scooted Jake up to the gunwale. I heard my voice scream *No,* but Jake went over with barely a splash. His head slipped under the water and never resurfaced. Coursey turned to me.

"You got the rifle on him?"

"Go ahead." Z spoke from behind the sight.

Coursey put his knife down and grabbed my shirt with both hands. "Come on, boy. Go easy now."

I felt myself being lifted. Coursey grunted with the effort. A deadweight of shackles and flesh. From my left I heard a dry spit in the night. Z stumbled sideways, then fell. Coursey glanced back at his boss. I wrapped my arms around his waist and took us both over the side.

I held Coursey close and kicked as hard as I could for the bottom. It took the cop a few seconds to realize my strategy. Then he began to thrash and claw, but my chains had become his own. Panic was eating away at his oxygen, and he knew it. We dropped into the darkness, faces inches apart. A single bubble escaped from his lips. Followed by a small stream. He made one last pull for the surface. I held fast. Then he coughed. And all the demons poured in.

I held his body until he stopped moving. Then I let go and watched him drift away. I was alone now. Still shackled, still dropping. Sarah flashed through my mind. Salt on her skin. Warm sunshine on her face. I opened my mouth a crack and took a final, watery breath.

46

The throat is your last line of defense. The palace guard, if you will, when it comes to drowning. No matter how hard you want to die, the throat will seal itself off when it detects water. A desperate effort to protect the lungs. It's not a lot of time, maybe another ten, twenty seconds before you're fully unconscious and the throat relaxes. In my case, however, it was enough. The diver found me at a depth of fifty feet and shared air to the surface. Then I was back on the deck of the Whaler, retching black water and tasting the bile of Lake Michigan. Michael Kelly stood nearby, watching quietly, a rifle with a scope in gloved hands.

I coughed and spit for ten minutes. The diver found some keys and unshackled me. Then he injected me with something, wrapped me in a blanket, and gave me a cup of broth. I sat up against the same engine cowling I'd been chained to a half hour earlier. The weather was still pea soup. Kelly squatted down beside me.

"How you feeling?"

"A little swim, but I'm okay." I smiled, but my hands were shaking. I reached up to touch my face and realized I was crying.

"Take it easy," Kelly said. "You're probably in a bit of shock."

I wiped my nose and took a sip of broth. "What happened?"

Kelly looked to the front. On cue, the Whaler rocked, and the fog lifted a touch. I could see two pairs of feet lined up on the deck, heels facing toward me. Z's green boots I recognized. The thick pair of black ones could only belong to Coursey.

"Both dead?" I said.

Kelly nodded. "I shot the woman. The divers got lucky and found the other one."

"How?" I said.

"Rodriguez told me to follow you. I was worried they might be watching me, so it was a loose tail. By the time I got to the beach house, they were already here. I saw the boat at the dock and told Rodriguez to get a dive team ready."

"What if they'd killed us in the house?"

"If I made a run at the house, chances are they would have killed you before I ever got there."

"So you took a chance?"

"We got lucky with the fog and the wind. Allowed us to stay fairly close. Once they chopped their engines, a couple of divers went into the water. The woman had the rifle, so I had to wait for my shot."

"Cut it kind of close."

Kelly shrugged. Then I remembered Jake. Kelly must have read it in my face.

"We got your buddy. He was in the water less than a minute. They're treating him on the other boat now."

I heard the muffled beat of an engine. A police boat cut through the murk and pulled up alongside. Rodriguez stepped across onto the Whaler, and the police boat motored away.

"How is he?" Rodriguez said.

Kelly tipped his head my way. "Asking a lot of questions, so I guess that's good."

Rodriguez took a seat. Kelly wandered up to the bow. We were still drifting. Still not headed anywhere special.

"Jake's gonna be fine," Rodriguez said. "They gave him some blood on the boat and stabilized him." He pointed off into the fog. "Taking him to the hospital now."

"Thanks, Detective."

"You're welcome." Rodriguez took out a pack of cigarettes and offered me one.

I shook my head. "Don't smoke."

"I don't either. Still, some days . . ." Rodriguez lit up. Kelly walked back. Rodriguez handed over the cigarettes, and Kelly disappeared again. Rodriguez took a single drag and tossed the butt into the water. "We've got a fucked-up situation here, Ian."

"I'm sorry."

"Not your fault. Hell, without you, where would we be? Not your fault at all."

The boat creaked as a wave passed beneath it.

"Why are we still out here?" I said. "Why aren't we headed in?"

"Good question." Rodriguez nodded toward the two sets of boots. "Guess we can start there."

"Z and Coursey?"

"What do we do with them? If we bring them in, we have to explain who shot them. And why."

"I can explain."

"Explain what?"

"Kelly had no choice. If he didn't shoot Z, I'd be dead. If . . ."

"I'm not talking about the details. That's not the problem at all."

"Then what is the problem?"

"The shed you guys cracked open. The cooler and those cabinets."

"You got a look?"

"A quick one." Rodriguez pulled out the black Moleskine notebook. "If we go public with what happened and give everyone the real reason why . . ."

"Then all the blackmail comes out. And a lot of people's lives are destroyed."

"That's right. Now if everything we find in that shed is true, I might not have any problem with letting it all come out in the wash. A handful of politicians get ruined. Maybe more than a handful, but so what? Thing is, some of that stuff . . . most of it probably . . . was the product of a frame. Either contrived evidence like your pal James Harrison, or a setup . . ."

"Like the one they caught me up in with Sarah."

"Something like that, yeah." Rodriguez studied my face. I knew where the cop was headed. The Needle Squad's blackmail ring might have started in Chicago, but now it reached all the way to Washington, into the highest levels of government. Anyone touched would be ruined. Whether they were guilty or innocent.

"What do we do?" I said.

"You three made it happen. You, Jake, and Sarah. Paid a pretty good price, too."

"So?"

"So what do you want to do?"

"I can't decide that, Detective."

Rodriguez grinned. "Who said you were gonna decide anything? I just want to know what you're thinking."

I shook my head. "I don't know."

"Good," Rodriguez said. "At your age, that's probably the right answer. We're gonna take you in and put you in a car. You'll be back in Evanston in a couple of hours. After that, you forget everything you saw today. The house, the shed. This boat. There'll be some questions, especially when the professor here doesn't show up for class. But you forget everything. Okay?"

"Okay."

Rodriguez searched my face. "Any questions, ask 'em now."

"Did you find Sally Finn?"

"She's in the beach house. Doesn't know her own name."

"There have to be more people involved in this."

"Best we can tell, only Z and Coursey knew the entire operation. Everyone else on the payroll just got bits and pieces. Police, prosecutors, a couple of reporters. Lots of hookers. We'll have a talk with them. Advise the cops and prosecutors to find a new line of work. Roll up the rest and keep 'em quiet."

"You think that'll work?"

"It's been done before."

"What are you going to do with them?" I gestured to the two pairs of boots on the deck.

"Let it go, son."

"You're going to drop me off, motor back here, and dump them in the lake."

Rodriguez stared at me. Kelly had reappeared at his shoulder.

"I can handle it, Detective."

"Fine. That's exactly what we're going to do."

"Then let's get on with it," I said.

Rodriguez circled his hand over his head once. Behind me the diesel turned over and began to hum. Forty minutes later, I was standing on the dock of Sally Finn's beach house, a cop close beside me. Rodriguez waved once as the Whaler slipped away from shore. Kelly stood beside him, staring at me. Then the boat was swallowed by the fog, and all I could hear was the beat of its engine.

47

In the end things went just about as Rodriguez said they would. Well, sort of.

Martin Coursey left a "note" for his two kids from a first, failed marriage. In it he told them he was leaving Chicago and wouldn't be returning. He asked them to forgive him. And if they couldn't forgive, at least forget.

As for Judy Zombrowski, what was left of her body washed up on the rocks along Lake Michigan's shoreline, not far from where the wreckage of the *Lady Elgin* came to rest. Her death was announced to the university as a "tragic accident." At Z's request, her remains were buried next to Rosina Rolland's in Calvary Cemetery. I was the only one who attended the ceremony. Along with Jake Havens.

Jake and I spent a lot of time together. He'd been in the hospital for a couple of weeks. The bullet hadn't done any permanent damage, but he'd lost a lot of blood. Jake told anyone who asked that it was an emergency appendectomy. I thought it might be hard to fool his family, but they only visited once and seemed to buy it. Neither of us had heard from Sarah since the hospital. She'd withdrawn from school, and all her e-mail bounced back. I grieved in the best way I knew, but maybe that was how it had to be for now. Just me and Jake. After all, no one else knew the full story. Not like Jake and I did. Well, sort of.

We sat in my car, stalled at a red light, on the corner of Roscoe and Halsted. Chicago's Boystown buzzed around us in a final burst of summer. Groups of men migrated across the street. Followed by even larger groups of women. People sat on curbs and stood on corners. Ahead of us a car doubled-parked as the driver rolled down his window and yelled into a club called Cocktail. A couple of men tumbled out of the place and jumped in the backseat. The stoplight flicked green, and we surged forward. Above us a guy leaned over a balcony and videotaped us with his iPhone.

I pulled into a 7-Eleven. A cop sat in the parking lot, sipping coffee and watching life in the side-view mirror. I slid into the space next to him. The cop backed up and left. Jake Havens looked over at me. He wasn't happy.

"Seriously, Joyce. What are we doing here?"

"I told you. It has something to do with the Harrison case."

"Yeah, and you told me it would all make sense once we got down here."

"It will."

"When?"

"Patience. You want something?"

He waved me away. I went into the store and came out with a couple of coffees. Jake took a sip. "You got any more sugar?"

I gave him a couple of packets and watched as he stirred one in. Jake had been out of the hospital for a month. The bullet had cost him twenty pounds and left him with a bloodless complexion. But Jake hadn't lost his intensity. And he hadn't lost his edge.

"How is it?" I said.

Jake took another sip of his coffee. "Getting better. So what's the deal?"

I glanced in my rearview mirror. A bar called Chasen's sat there. Its windows were swung open to the street, and the high stools were packed with patrons. Another cop car cruised past. No one in Chasen's took any notice.

"I know who Skylar Wingate's killer is." I spoke softly, almost reluctantly. "He broke into my house a couple of months ago. I have a security camera in the basement. Got three minutes of him on tape."

"The killer broke into your house?"

"Yes."

"And you've got him on tape?"

"Yes."

Jake studied me closely. "Fine. Let's take a look."

I shook my head.

"Why not?" Jake leaned forward and put his coffee in the holder between us. Best I could tell, he'd already drunk a quarter.

"You see that bar behind us?" I said.

He turned and looked.

"I've been up and down this strip for the last month, flashing this guy's picture. Finally got a hit last week."

"In there?"

"He's been in there the last three weekends running. Looking for his next victim."

"And why should I believe this guy's our killer?"

"He is, Jake."

"That's it?"

"For now."

"Fuck you, Joyce."

We lapsed back into silence. Chatter from the street drifted through an open window.

"Have the cops seen your tape?" Jake said.

"I figured we should talk first."

"You figured wrong. Call Rodriguez."

I took out my phone and placed it on the dash.

Jake looked at it. "You don't think I'll call."

"It's your choice."

"You're not the one who took the bullet, Joyce. You think I want another?"

"That's why it's your choice."

He picked up his coffee and took another sip. "What is it you want to do?"

"Find the guy who killed Skylar Wingate."

"You sound pretty sure of yourself."

"I am."

He shook his head and stared straight ahead. I turned up the radio. He turned it off.

"What will we do with him? Once we have him?"

"You know the answer to that. You've always known." I put the car into gear and pulled out of the lot. We circled the block and eased into a shallow alley that dead-ended at a dark and deserted laundromat. From the alley, we had a direct view of Chasen's.

"You're wrong," Jake said.

"About what?"

"I don't want to hurt this guy. Or whatever you have planned. I never did."

I picked up my phone. "Then make the call."

Across the street, a man stood in the gutter, hawking a *Streetwise* in front of the bar. On the other side of Halsted, a bum wearing a Cubs hat crouched at a bus stop and watched the crowds drift by. A cop at the corner talked to a skinny black kid.

"I know what's going on." Jake's voice carried the burden of confidence, which told me he knew nothing. Or at least not everything he thought.

"What's going on, Jake?"

"You really want to hear it?"

I half turned in my seat. "Maybe I'd better."

He licked his lips. It was the first time I'd ever seen Jake Havens nervous. And I knew what he was going to say next. "It started with the cord used to strangle Wingate. The one we saw in the photos."

"What about it?" I said.

"It looked like something you'd find in a school. At least it seemed that way to me. So I went back to Wingate's grammar school and took a hard look at the staff. I got hold of some old payroll records and put together a list of names."

"Sounds like a lot of work."

"I came across a janitor named Edward Cooper. Left the school six months after Skylar was killed. Skipped town altogether a year and a half after that. I was able to trace Cooper to Nevada. He raped a boy out there and was sentenced to twenty-five years in prison. They released him seven months ago."

"You got a description of Cooper?"

"There's more."

I nodded. Jake Havens was number one in his class at the University of Chicago. Of course, there was more.

"This guy had a family in Chicago back in the day. Wife and two boys. Twins."

I glanced over. Jake's eyes were wide and shiny. "Let me guess," I said. "The mom's maiden name was Joyce. And she named her twins Ian and Matthew."

"You've known all along."

"Edward Cooper was my stepfather. He lived with us until I was ten. And, yes, he killed those kids. The three back in the day and the two now. That's why we're here tonight."

"I don't understand." The words came out thick and slow. Jake looked down at his coffee and back up at me. I took the cup from his hands and cranked back his seat. He tried to remain upright, but failed miserably.

"I couldn't take a chance on you, Jake. You're just too goddamn smart." I threw the car keys on the floor. "When you wake up, drive yourself back to Evanston. Go straight to bed 'cuz you're gonna have a mean headache. I'm sorry about that. And I'm sorry about the rest."

Jake's lips moved, but no words came out. I put my hand on his shoulder and waited until his eyes had closed. Then I took the remains of his coffee and dumped it in the gutter. I locked the car and left my classmate, unconscious, in the alley.

Half a block down Roscoe, I had a van parked in an empty lot. I found it and checked to make sure I had everything I needed. Then I walked back up toward the lights of Halsted. From the darkness of the side street, I studied the intersection. The cop was still on the corner. The man selling *Streetwise* across from him. The bum in the Cubs hat at the bus stop. And all the rest, sitting and drinking, enjoying their night. I felt the edge of the knife tucked into the belt of my pants, cold against my belly. Then I walked toward the lights.

48

I watched him hunt for an hour. His genius was preparation and patience. My job was to stay close yet remain invisible. To my surprise, I was pretty good at it. Like stepfather, I guessed, like stepson.

I took him in the very heart of the night. The bars were letting out. Sidewalks swollen with people. He was intent on his prey. A young boy, maybe thirteen, alone, wearing a black T-shirt, black jeans, and featuring spiky blue hair. He'd been watching the boy, on and off, for the better part of an hour. Now the boy was heading toward an alley, probably for a smoke or a piss. My stepfather started to follow. We bumped shoulders as he passed, knocking him off stride and into an empty doorway. I moved with him, finding the flesh in his thigh and pressing the needle home. His hand gripped my wrist, but it was too late. I got one look at the rim of yellow in his eyes, maybe a flicker of recognition. Then the eyes fluttered shut, and he slumped against me. I picked up his Cubs hat and helped him down the street, telling anyone who asked he was drunk. No one cared about a bum. Least of all, the cops. Less than a minute later, I had him in the back of the van, strapped down, mouth taped, hands and feet cuffed. I wanted to look at him, but there was no time. And my heart was suddenly popping in my throat. So I climbed into the front of the van, turned over the engine, and headed back to Evanston. It was so much easier than I ever could have imagined. The beast conjured far worse than the one slain.

"What do you remember about this place?" I said.

He blinked and tried to move. The strap across his forehead forced him to look at me.

"You remember that?" I pointed to a square hole cut into the floor. His eyes flicked down and back up.

"You're in the basement. Your old basement."

There was contempt in his gaze. Or maybe it was just boredom. I gripped the black handle and cranked a notch on the rope that held his right leg fast. The tendons in his leg pulled tight.

"I got new ropes, but it's the same winch and pulley. Oiled them up. Same table, too." I rapped my knuckles against it. Then I flicked at the flex-cuffs that pinned his hands and left leg to the wood. "I could have hooked you up all around, but you know that."

I reached for the handle and cracked another notch. My stepfather bit at the gag in his mouth. His right leg twisted outward at the knee and ankle.

"You're probably enjoying this," I said. The cords in his neck swelled as he struggled to lift his head off the table.

"You want to talk?" I made a move to remove his gag, then pulled back. "Fuck you."

I took it up two more notches and was rewarded with a heavy grunt through the gag.

"That's four notches. I remember because that was when Matthew screamed. I screamed with him. You turned up the radio. Then you cranked it five more times."

I put my hand on the handle. Edward Cooper's mind was already broken. Why not a leg? I leaned into the job. A voice whispered from across the room. At first I thought it was my own. The pathetic ghost of a boy. Watching his twin being murdered. And wondering why it wasn't him. Then Sarah Gold stepped out of the shadows. And saved my life.

49

She stood there, arms wrapped around her waist, cupping her elbows like she was holding the pieces of herself together.

"Go away, Sarah."

"If you're going to do this, you'll do it with me watching."

"You think I won't?"

"I was there tonight, Ian. In Boystown."

My hand slipped off the handle. The pressure eased back a notch. "Why?"

"Jake thought we had things under control. I agreed with him. Turns out we were both wrong."

"No kidding."

"Jake's fine. In case you were wondering."

"It was just a sedative. I wouldn't hurt him."

"I believe you." Sarah edged closer. For the first time I noticed a yellow envelope clutched in her hand.

"What's that?"

"X-rays. From Matthew."

A small sigh escaped from my lips and I stumbled back from the table.

"It was Jake's idea," she said. "He pulled your brother's old school records. That led us to the hospital reports. A broken wrist. Three ribs.

A cracked sternum. Two days ago, Detective Rodriguez got a court order to exhume your brother's body."

I sagged to the floor and felt the cold run of bricks against my spine. Sarah's voice cut through the black smoke of time and memory.

"Matthew's body was swollen when they pulled him out of the lake. No one ever bothered to check his legs. Why would they when everyone thought he'd drowned?"

I pulled out the X-rays and held them in my lap. Splintered pieces of bone. The whites of Matthew's eyes. High, thin screams.

"I remember when the first leg went," I said. Sarah made a small sound in her throat. "My stepfather acted like he'd broken his favorite toy. And there was no putting it back together. So he broke the other one." I snapped my fingers. "Just like that.

"He kept a small launch in a slip down at the lake. Rolled Matthew up in a carpet and hauled him out in that. Then he threw him overboard and watched him drown." I slipped the X-rays back into their sleeve and gave Sarah a wintry grin. "You wonder what I was doing tonight? I was hunting him. Before he hurt anyone else."

She was close now. Close enough that I could smell her skin. Feel her breath on my face. I took out my mother's letter and placed it on top of Matthew's X-rays. "My mom left me this when she passed."

Sarah unfolded the letter and ran her eyes over it. I kept talking.

"She made sure I knew Cooper was getting out of jail. Told me I needed to do something. She hadn't done a damn thing to protect her kids, but now I needed to do something."

Sarah glanced up from her reading, but I waved her on.

"She told me about Skylar Wingate and the others. About the hole in the cellar where Cooper kept his trophies. Rings. Wallets. Clippings of hair. The piece of Skylar's shirt."

"So it was you who sent the shirt to Jake?"

"Z's seminar had access to the old case files. I thought if I got you all interested, we might stumble on a lead, something that might help me find him."

"Instead, we found the Needle Squad."

"I never meant for you to get hurt, Sarah. You or Jake."

She flinched once, then folded up the letter and returned it to its envelope. "What about tonight?"

"What about it?"

"What did you have planned?"

I took a long, cool breath and glanced across the room, at the man strapped to the table. "I wanted to kill him. Until there wasn't any killing left."

"It's wrong, Ian."

"You don't know what I know. You don't hear what I hear."

"He'll pay for what he did in a court of law."

"And you think that's enough?"

"It has to be. Otherwise, he's already won."

There was a pause, then a footfall. Michael Kelly stepped into a pool of pale yellow light. I turned back to Sarah. "Your guardian angel?"

Her fingers grazed my cheek. "Something like that."

I climbed to my feet and walked toward my stepfather. His eyes tracked mine. Christened me a coward. Once a coward, always one. I brushed past the table and headed for the stairs, Kelly at my side. As we walked, his hand fell over the black handle and cracked it hard, cranking the pulleys tight, and snapping Edward Cooper's tibia just below the knee. I heard the high-pitched keen through the gag. Kelly gripped my arm with his other hand and kept me moving toward the stairs. When we got to the top, he pushed me through the door and closed it behind me.

50

My stepfather got his day in court. Six life sentences, to be served con-
secutively, with no chance of parole. He'd die in a hundred-year-old
maximum-security prison, a half hour from the Illinois-Missouri state
line. I saw him for what I hoped was the last time at his sentencing.
He kept his head down for most of the hearing and declined to speak.
When it was finished, he stood, right leg in a soft splint, and waited for
the deputies to hook him up. As they worked on his chains, he took a
look around the courtroom. I wanted to walk away, but stayed where I
was. He saw me, moved past, then came back. His face was shrunken
and pitted; his hair slicked back to a dull sheen. He mouthed some
words, but I couldn't make them out. Then he held out his shackles. I
took a look at the thick hands, wrists, arms, then up into the eyes that
had terrified me as a child. I wanted to see a monster, but all I saw was
an old man. I wanted to feel anger, but all I felt was sadness. Maybe
Sarah was right. Maybe I was done.

I met her at Mustard's Last Stand. We ordered a basket of fries and
sat outside.

"How was it?" she said.

"It was. He got his time and now he's gone."

"Are you glad you went?"

"I guess so. It feels like something. A passage, maybe, of some sort."

"Things will get better."

"I know."

Sarah's hand found mine, and our fingers wove themselves together. "You want to talk about it?"

"Not really. Not today." A breeze passed between us, and we both felt the chill. I glanced at my watch. "What time's your flight?"

"Three hours."

"I've never been out there," I said, "but I bet you'll like it."

"Berkeley's got a great program in communications. And San Francisco's close."

"Yeah."

She tipped her head and caught my eyes. "What is it?"

"Nothing."

"Ian?"

"I'm gonna miss you." The words felt naked, vulnerable.

"You'll visit."

"It won't be the same."

"And that's a bad thing?" She smiled. I laughed. And life moved a little. But not very far.

"I'll be back in December," she said.

"Mistake."

"We already talked about this. And I've decided."

When Marty Coursey broke into Sarah's apartment, he had an accomplice. Another cop who made the mistake of leaving a clean thumbprint on a mirror in Sarah's bedroom. Rodriguez told her they could take care of the guy. Make it hurt without him ever seeing the inside of a courtroom. But Sarah wanted her own day in court. And wasn't going to be deterred.

"Do you know why, Ian?"

"You know I don't."

"Because I believe in the system. I believe in working within the system. Even if it's imperfect. Even if the bad guy sometimes goes free. That's why I want this man charged. And I want a jury to hear the evidence against him."

"And what if he walks?"

"Come what may, I'll face my demons and be free of them. Just like you did today."

"Didn't you once tell me you can't escape your past?"

"Exactly. So learn to embrace it."

I shook my head. The woman always had an answer. "I'm gonna miss you, Sarah."

"Quit saying that. You'll visit. Jake, too. Where is he, by the way?"

"He told me you guys did your good-byes last night."

"We had dinner. Let me guess. He's working?"

"Twenty-four/seven."

Skylar Wingate had driven Jake Havens back to a place he probably never should have left—the law. He'd taken a job with the Cook County Public Guardian's office and would spend his life fighting for kids no one else cared about. I couldn't think of anyone better.

"Are you two going out this week?" Sarah said.

"We're supposed to get a drink tonight."

"Good."

I grabbed at a couple of fries in the basket and checked my watch again. "You about ready?"

A sigh. "I guess."

Neither of us moved. A car zipped past on Central. Then another.

"I'm not gonna tell you I miss you again."

She leaned in and kissed me. "I've got something for you." She pulled up her bag and took out a small white envelope. "You remember that night on the beach?"

"Sure."

A Sarah smile. "Not that part . . . although that was great. You remember when you told me a person's reach should never exceed his grasp?"

"You mean when I misquoted Browning and you corrected me? I remember."

"This one's from Washington Irving. I read it the other day and thought of you."

She handed me the envelope. I looked at the loops and curves in my name and thought about the hand that had formed them. One that cared for me without fear or condition. Then I opened the envelope and took out the single page inside. I read it under the dying light.

There is a sacredness in tears. They are not the mark of weakness, but of power. They speak more eloquently than ten thousand tongues. They are messengers of overwhelming grief . . . and unspeakable love.

"Don't be afraid of your tears, Ian. And I promise I won't be afraid of mine. Deal?"

"For life."

I kissed her again. She teared up. And we laughed at the stupid irony. Then it was late, and we thought for sure she'd miss her flight. So we bundled our feelings in with her bags and packed it all away in my car. And then we were off to O'Hare. It was the end of things as they were. And the beginning of whatever was to come.

ACKNOWLEDGMENTS

Northwestern's Medill School of Journalism is the setting and inspiration for a lot of this book. I'd like to thank everyone in the Medill community, especially my students, whose unique voices inspired me to write *The Innocence Game*. I'd be remiss if I did not also take note of Medill's Innocence Project. In 1999, it was one of the first to shine a light on the problem of wrongful convictions and was instrumental in the suspension and eventual abolition of the death penalty in Illinois. The Innocence Seminar described in this book is entirely fictional and in no way resembles the real-life Innocence Project at Medill. Ian, Sarah, and Jake, however, do represent what we see in Medill classrooms every day: the intellectual curiosity and desire to uncover the truth at any price.

I'd also like to thank my agent, David Gernert; my editor, Jordan Pavlin; and all the folks at Knopf and Vintage / Black Lizard who have provided such amazing support for my novels. Thanks to Garnett Kilberg Cohen, Chicago writer and professor at Columbia College, for her support and impeccable advice.

Thanks to my friends and family for all their love and support. Finally, thank you, Mary Frances. I can't imagine doing any of it without you.

A NOTE ABOUT THE AUTHOR

Michael Harvey is the author of *The Chicago Way, The Fifth Floor, The Third Rail* and *We All Fall Down*, as well as a journalist and documentary producer. His work has won numerous national and international awards, including multiple news Emmys, two Primetime Emmy nominations and an Academy Award nomination. He holds a law degree with honours from Duke University, a master's degree in journalism from Northwestern University and a bachelor's degree in classical languages from Holy Cross College. He lives in Chicago.

www.michaelharveybooks.com
Follow Michael Harvey on Twitter @thechicagoway

This book was set in Monotype Dante, a typeface designed by Giovanni Mardersteig (1892–1977). Modeled on the Aldine type used for Pietro Cardinal Bembo's treatise *De Aetna* in 1495, Dante is a modern interpretation of the venerable face.